The Woman Next Door

Mukōda Kuniko

Translated by

A. Reid Monroe-Sheridan

KURODAHAN PRESS

2021

The Woman Next Door by Mukōda Kuniko

Original book publication:
Tonari no Onna, Bungeishunju Ltd., Japan, 1981.
English rights arranged through Bungeishunju Ltd., Japan.

First publication information:

隣りの女 (Tonari no Onna), *Sunday Mainichi*, May 10, 1981
幸福 (Kōfuku), *All Yomimono*, Sept. 1980
胡桃の部屋 (Kurumi no Heya), *All Yomimono*, March, 1981
下駄 (Geta), *Bessatsu Bungei Shunjū*, No. 153, 1980
春が来た (Haru ga Kita), *All Yomimono*, Oct. 1981

Cover: Ramona Russu

FG-JP0067A2

ISBN: 978-4-909473-18-9

KURODAHAN.COM

Contents

The Woman Next Door

SEWING MACHINES DON'T LIE. They are just appliances, and yet they speak with greater candor about the women who use them than those women do themselves.

This was just about the time of day when she would hear the voices next door. She really didn't want to hear them and thought she ought to sew twice as hard to drown them out. Yet the sewing machine dutifully made its usual sound: *clack-clack-clack.*

Feeling as though her true intention had been exposed, Sachiko threw herself into the sewing. Who cared if the thing broke—it was borrowed anyway.

Sachiko was a subcontractor, earning twelve hundred yen per blouse. Her husband brought home a good monthly salary and they didn't have any kids yet, so it wasn't like she had to work herself to death. But it would be a waste to just loaf around all day. Besides, she wanted to save some more money.

But those thoughts just couldn't keep Sachiko's mind from the wall behind her. She lived in an inexpensive apartment with two bedrooms and a combined kitchen and dining room. There was a well-known Western painting hanging on one of the white walls of the six-tatami-mat living and dining space. The painting, a reproduction of course, was positioned directly behind Sachiko's back as her foot rested on the pedal of the sewing machine. And the voices came from behind that painting.

Suddenly, there was a violent noise, something like a glass bowl being hurled at the wall. Male and female voices arguing. Sachiko's sewing machine seemed to slow down by itself.

"Don't fuck around with me! What do you mean 'the right time'? Tell me his name! I'll beat him to death!" It was the man's voice.

"If you're going to get violent, leave! There is no other man! What are you doing? Let go of me!" The woman's voice was also fierce.

The sounds of pushing and shoving followed. And then, "Be careful of the glass." The woman's voice took on a sweet, supplicating tone.

Sachiko left the machine and approached the wall. She put her ear up against it.

"Hey, be careful of the glass," said the woman.

"It's fine."

"Just be careful, all right?"

"Mineko."

"Oh, Nobee."

Mineko was the name of the woman who lived next door, the *mama-san* of a Japanese-style snack bar where women served drinks and small dishes to male customers. Nobu—or "Nobee"—was a young man who had the look of a construction foreman. He had started coming by recently. Sachiko heard his thick, husky voice almost every other day, so she recognized him immediately.

Her neighbor's rough, quick breathing intensified, and soon the wall began to shake lightly. Sachiko was a little surprised to find herself matching the pace of her own breathing to theirs. She felt hot, but surely that had nothing to do with what was happening next door. She told herself it was because she was still wearing her spring clothes in this warm summer weather.

The whole thing was manageable up to that point. But then Sachiko was surprised to see, in the full-length mirror next to the sewing machine, the strange, twisted shape of her own body as she leaned against the wall and pressed her ear to it to hear the hints from next door. She straightened abruptly and adjusted the picture on the wall. It didn't look particularly tilted, but readjusting it had become a habit of hers.

WHEN SACHIKO LEFT HER apartment, shopping basket in hand, she found a plastic bag full of garbage right at her feet. The *mama-san* next door had probably put it in front of her own door and the wind had pushed it over to Sachiko's. She pinched part of the bag between her fingertips and flung it back in front of the *mama-san*'s door. There was nothing special about this trash from next door, but Sachiko felt that it was especially filthy.

There wasn't much greenery in her neighborhood, yet the street carried the scent of leaves.

I'd rather smell flowers than this suffocating foliage, thought Sachiko. She was pretty sure that last year the area around her apartment had smelled of sweet olives. But even in this neighborhood, houses with gardens and undeveloped land were disappearing year after year, as apartments stacked like matchboxes took their place.

Sachiko's apartment was a five-minute walk from the Ōizumi-gakuen Station on the Seibu-Ikebukuro train line. She and her husband Shūtarō would probably be able to live in a better apartment complex if they moved out to Mitama, but Shūtarō said that commuting for more than an hour was too much of an inconvenience, so their rent wasn't cheap. Sachiko wasn't clear on whether the distance would be "inconvenient" for Shūtarō's career success or just for his evening socializing. But at this point they didn't have any kids, so she was able to keep them out of debt through her part-time job.

Sachiko glared sidelong at the butcher shop and walked into the fish store. She bought a single serving of red snapper scrap meat, scrutinizing her two options before having her choice wrapped for her.

A housewife who looked to be about Sachiko's age came in with a child of about two and a half. Sachiko patted his head and smiled at him. *So if he'd been born, he would be this big now, huh?*

Sachiko had kept working until she received her year-end bonus, and then she'd miscarried. Maybe the air conditioning in her office was to blame. She'd been sure it was a boy, and for a while it was painful for her to so much as look at any baby boy. Her parents had told her that it's best to have your first child before you turn thirty, so she took her weak health as an opportunity to quit her job and spend her days in a kind of "child-waiting."

She passed by the bookstore and the record store and went into the greengrocer. Only on rare occasions would Sachiko buy a book or listen to a record. Shūtarō was the same way.

She picked up some chrysanthemum leaves and shiitake mushrooms, and took a one-thousand-yen bill, folded into eighths, out of her red coin purse. The greengrocer's smudged mirror reflected Sachiko's expressionless face. She was only twenty-eight and yet her face lacked vitality—maybe because she didn't wear makeup. Making ends meet on her husband's salary, preparing their food, taking care of the cleaning and laundry, her sewing work—these chores brought her an acute awareness of the passing days. From time to time she would let out a deep sigh.

Sachiko couldn't say if this was happiness, but she wasn't particularly unhappy either. Then again, these days she was strangely irritated by the face of Shōtoku Taishi on the ten-thousand-yen bill.

Sachiko bought a mountain of the toilet paper that was on sale. As she finished her climb up the outdoor staircase of her apartment building, she found the door next to hers open. She bumped into the man as he was leaving.

As he passed by Sachiko, his face was so grim that it seemed as though his exchange with her neighbor—him calling her "Mineko" in a sweet voice and her calling him "Nobee" in return—must all have been a lie.

Mineko herself had opened her door halfway and was seeing the man off. Her sweaty hair was plastered to her face. When Mineko didn't put on makeup, her murky complexion gave her a sickly appearance, but when she did make the effort it transformed her into someone else. She must have been seven or eight years older than Sachiko, yet even her languid movements and the creases in the corners of her eyes suggested a certain sensuality.

Without saying anything to Mineko, Sachiko entered her own apartment and resumed her sewing. When Sachiko wanted to talk to someone, the sewing machine became her partner in conversation. She vented her anger and spilled her complaints to it. And when she calmed down, the machine was a pillow for her to nap on.

HALF-DREAMING, SACHIKO ONCE AGAIN heard the voice of the woman next door.

"Where is Mt. Tanigawa again?"

A man's voice answered, "It's on the border of the Jōetsu region in Gunma Prefecture."

"So then it's on the Jōetsu train line from Ueno in Tokyo?"

"Ueno. Oku. Akabane. Urawa. Ōmiya. Miyahara. Ageo. Okegawa. Kitamoto. Kōnosu. Fukiage." The man's voice was soft but it had a nice ring to it. He spoke the station names one by one, as if he were reading a poem.

It wasn't a dream. The voices were clearly coming from the other side of the wall, from the room next door.

"Gyōda. Kumagaya. Kagohara. Fukaya. Okabe. Honjō. Jimbohara. Jimbohara." The man's voice faltered.

It wasn't the usual man. This wasn't the thick, rasping voice of the foreman Mineko called "Nobee." This voice was more profound. Sachiko stood up, enticed.

"Jimbohara. Shinmachi. Kuragano. Takasaki. Ino. Shin-Maebashi. Gunma-Sōja. Yagihara. Shibukawa. Shikishima. Tsukuda. Iwamoto. Numata. Gokan. Kamimoku. Minakami. Yubiso. Doai."

Finished, the man let out a large sigh. The woman giggled like a cooing pigeon and nestled up to the man.

"You remember it so well."

"When I go to climb Mt. Tanigawa, I can't ride the express because it's just such a waste. I take the local train from Ueno and approach the mountain little by little."

Sachiko's body was approaching the wall little by little.

"When I think about gradually closing in on the mountain, no matter how many times I've climbed it, I get this pounding in my chest like it's my first time. When I get off at Doai Station and I look up at the mountain, I can feel myself getting flustered and flushed in the face."

"You're like a little boy." Sachiko felt the excitement in Mineko's voice. "Is it a pretty mountain?"

"Every mountain is pretty. Doesn't matter which mountain it is, when you see them from far away they all look the same. But when you climb them carefully, step by step, they're different. The foot of the mountain has this gentle slope."

"That tickles!"

"There are hollows, hidden away in unexpected places."

"I said that tickles."

"There are places in the sunlight. Places in shadow. Dry places. Moist places. And they all look as if they're breathing."

Sachiko was leaning up against the wall with her legs stretched out to the side. She began to stroke herself softly. Part of her skirt was upturned, her legs peeking out. The sunset, filtering through her window, drew a map of light and shadow on her body.

The man's voice was a little muffled and sweeter than before.

"When you see mountains in the morning, they look divine."

"When you see them in the afternoon?" The woman's voice was serious.

"They look sturdy."

"When you see them at night?"

"They're threatening. Scary."

Sachiko heard the woman giggle. Slowly, the wall began to shake.

"Please, say the station names one more time."

"Ueno. Oku. Akabane. Urawa. Ōmiya. Miyahara. Ageo. Okegawa. Kitamoto. Kōnosu. Fukiage. Gyōda. Kumagaya. Kagohara. Fukaya."

Sachiko's earlobes felt hot. Her breathing was strained. She felt an intoxication circulating through her.

"Okabe. Honjō. Jimbohara. Shinmachi. Kuragano. Takasaki. Ino. Shin-Maebashi. Gunma-Sōja. Yagihara. Shibukawa. Shikishima. Tsukuda. Iwamoto. Numata. Gokan. Kamimoku. Minakami. Yubiso. Doai."

Sachiko closed her eyes tightly. The backs of her eyelids were turning red—she was climbing up to the top of a mountain. Soon she was at the peak and all of her strength evaporated, as if she had died and couldn't move.

Sunset was changing into dusk. Sachiko could hear some rowdy children below the apartment, but she continued to lean against the wall. The blouse she had started on was lying atop the sewing machine. The clock struck five.

Sachiko came to her senses at the sound of the door being opened. She had been dreaming shallowly in that reclined state but now jumped to her feet and peered into the hallway.

Mineko was wearing a nightgown and standing on the outdoor staircase, one hand raised. The man was heading home. He was young, dressed in a worn-out raincoat. His back was to her, so Sachiko couldn't see his face. As if to answer Mineko's raised hand he raised his own and waved it a few times without turning around. It was a beautiful hand, tapered in shape, a hand that didn't perform manual labor.

This was obviously another man. Mineko stood still, gazing at the man's back. It was partly the effect of the evening light, but Mineko looked more alluring than when she had seen off Nobee.

"Um, about the money I lent you for the gas bill . . ." Sachiko tried to say the words, but they wouldn't come. She stood silently, feeling absolutely pathetic. The word "defeat" flickered before her eyes.

"OUR WATER TASTES BEST."

Her husband Shūtarō always drank a cup of water when he got home.

What he probably meant was that their water was better than the water at his office, better than the water at the mah-jongg parlor, better than the water at the string of bars he went to when he did his "networking."

"Well, it all comes from the same Tokyo Water Bureau," Sachiko would usually retort. But this evening her thoughts were in another place, so her husband's comment went unanswered.

"I told you not to wait for me when I'm going to be late, didn't I?" He was complaining about the untouched meal for two on the dinner table. "It's not like I want to come home late. My boss keeps making me."

He mimicked stacking up mah-jongg tiles. "One person can't just leave the game on his own. It's like what they say about the shamisen."

"The shamisen? Like this?" Sachiko mimed playing the instrument. Shūtarō looked shocked.

"Wow, you really don't know anything. In mah-jongg, 'shamisen' means confusing your opponents by bluffing or tricking them. It's that whole environment—you know how we all shoot the bull when we play mah-jongg."

"Oh, that."

"That's when we all cut loose and let each other know what we're really thinking. A businessman doesn't work from only nine to five."

"This happens at the mah-jongg parlor?"

"I can't bring my colleagues home, can I? My salary is low and my wife works a part-time job at home."

"I don't work because of your salary. I just have extra time and I don't want to waste it."

"Then put this stuff away before I get home."

Until then, Sachiko had always cleaned up the blouses she was working on, but this time the blouse was still laid out on the sewing machine. As Sachiko started to put it away, Shūtarō said, "Leave it. Don't make all that fuss right in front of me. I was just saying."

As Shūtarō yawned and changed into his pajamas, Sachiko brought up the topic she just couldn't resist talking about.

"You know that person next door?"

"Next door? Oh, from the snack bar. The *mama-san* hired by the bar's manager?"

"She's something else." Sachiko raised one of her thumbs to indicate a man. "Two guys. And both in one day."

"Cut it out."

Sticking his own thumb up, Shūtarō made a disgusted face.

"Women shouldn't gesture like this. It's not something a nice girl would do."

"So, what should I do then?"

"Why don't you just say the words with your mouth?"

"Then should I say 'a man'? That sounds kind of dirty too."

"So what's the story with these men?"

"There are two of them."

"That's not so strange. It would be a big deal if she was married, but for women in her line of work, two or three guys—"

"Even so, I thought that the guy who looks like a construction foreman, the one who always comes around noon, was here today. But when I came back from my errands around three and started working with the sewing machine, I heard a different voice. It wasn't the usual guy's voice."

"Is this how you spend your time all day?"

Sachiko flinched a little and said in a small voice, "I just hear them without even listening."

"Don't associate with weirdos."

Letting out another big yawn, Shūtarō climbed into his futon. Sachiko dimmed the lights, but she didn't want to go back to the kitchen just then.

"Have you ever climbed Mt. Tanigawa?"

"Mt. Tanigawa?" Shūtarō yawned again. "Never. Why are you asking me all of a sudden?"

"Can you name the train stops from Ueno to Tanigawa?"

"I've come back from eight hours of hard work and then networking during our mah-jongg game. I don't have time for some dumb quiz."

He turned his face away with an impatient expression and immediately started snoring.

THE NEXT DAY, WHEN Sachiko was on her way back home from delivering some blouses, she made the rare decision to buy a record. She wanted something very solemn, and she settled on Bach's Requiem Mass.

As soon as Sachiko got back to her apartment, she put the record on at high volume. While she was changing clothes, the wall entered her thoughts. She approached it, listening for a sound, but she couldn't hear anything. She lowered the volume of the record and listened again, then stopped the record entirely and listened again. But there were no sounds at all.

"You're acting stupid." Just as Sachiko burst into laughter and clapped herself on the head there was a knock at the door. The building manager was standing there. She was a woman of about seventy.

Without any warning, she said, "Ma'am, are you busy right now?"

If Sachiko wasn't busy, would she make the short trip to Ikebukuro? While the *mama-san* next door was standing by the mailbox and chatting before she went to work, she'd accidentally left the keys to her snack bar there. She had business to take care of at the moment and couldn't come back home to pick up the keys, so she'd asked if someone could bring them to her.

"If I had the spare time, I'd do it myself. I actually wanted to get a look at her bar. She keeps telling me it's too small and that's why she misses her rent payments. Ma'am, get a good look at it for me." She gave Sachiko a map and the keys, and Sachiko set out.

The snack bar was called Puzzle. It was a basement-level unit in an alley full of bars near the main entrance of Ikebukuro station. Sachiko expected that when she climbed down the stairs, Mineko would be standing in front of the bar, but instead Mineko came out from inside the bar laughing.

"Thanks, but it worked out." Mineko apologized; she had thought that the bartender was off today, but he showed up so she didn't need the keys anymore. She had called back to tell the building manager, but Sachiko had already set off by that point. After she paid Sachiko back for the cab fare, would Sachiko please stay for a drink? Mineko offered her a chair.

It was a shabby bar that couldn't comfortably fit even ten people. The rough-looking bartender was peeling celery. There was only one other customer, a young man sitting alone at the end of the counter, working on a Rubik's Cube. Sachiko asked for coffee, but Mineko quickly gave her a whiskey and water and smiled.

"I bet you can handle this."

"Thank you." Sachiko bowed her head courteously but then realized that the gesture wasn't right for a place like this. The man at the end of the counter glanced at her. The two women framed the counter on opposite sides: a well-dressed and thoroughly made-up woman and a woman wearing no makeup at all. Across from those long, red nails, Sachiko's short, unmanicured nails looked plain and worn from housework. Sachiko gathered her nerve and gulped down the whiskey. She choked violently. Mineko thumped her on the back.

Sachiko's throat always tensed when she got nervous. Choking was a habit of hers.

"I always screw up when it matters most." Sachiko mentioned how she would get stomachaches whenever she took tests in school and how a pimple showed up on the tip of her nose just on the day when she was taking her formal matchmaking photographs.

"And last year was like that too. When it came time to leave for Paris—my friends also work part-time jobs at home and we always work really hard, so we agreed we should do something extravagant for once—I got my passport ready and everything, but then I got appendicitis."

"You couldn't go?"

"That's the kind of thing that happens to me."

Mineko's eyes, black tinged with blue, suddenly smiled amiably.

"I had appendicitis too."

"Recently?"

"A long time ago."

Sachiko was pleased. "Mine is about this big." She indicated the four-centimeter scar with her fingers.

"Mine." Mineko did the same, but hers was two centimeters longer.

"Whoa, that's big."

"Well, it was a country doctor, and this was a long time ago."

"Oh, so he probably sewed it up then."

"What, did you get yours stapled?" As soon as Mineko said it, her expression froze. There was a customer standing near the door. It was that man. The construction foreman, Nobee, who always came by the apartment.

"Welcome to Puzzle," said Mineko. Her voice was suddenly formal as she ducked under the counter to the other side. She said to the bartender, "Keep an eye on things for a moment, okay?" and then she leaned into Nobee and they exited the bar.

Sachiko hurriedly drank her whiskey and water.

Judging by the state of things this morning, Shūtarō would probably be late again tonight, but Sachiko still needed to prepare dinner. What should she make?

The young man at the edge of the counter was turning the rotary dial on a pink telephone.

"Is this Professor Takechi's residence?"

Sachiko was stunned.

"It's Asada from Hōbundō, the store. We're handling the picture frames—yes, Asada. About the timing, it's going to be two or three days late."

It was unmistakably that voice.

"No, that's all right. Number eighty and number sixty. The still-life shots. Those pictures, and the rose, number forty."

After that, the conversation turned to the arrangements for the deadline. To Sachiko, his voice sounded like music.

"Shinmachi. Kuragano. Takasaki. Ino. Shin-Maebashi. Gunma-Sōja." She could hear his voice from before. It was hard to breathe. She gulped down the rest of her whiskey and water and stood, setting her glass down with a *clunk*. Just then the man hung up the phone. He stared right back at Sachiko, as if her strong gaze on him had made him suspicious. He was perhaps a year or two past thirty, with handsome features, but his eyes were gloomy. With that, Sachiko left the bar.

As Sachiko was exiting from the basement to street level, she found Mineko and Nobee pushing and shoving each other on the landing of the staircase. Nobee pushed Mineko into the wall with his body.

"I can't stand it." He was on the verge of tears. Mineko's face was stiff. Sachiko froze when she saw a flash of light near Nobee's right hand. But when

Mineko noticed Sachiko, she put her arms around Nobee gently and called out to Sachiko, "Oh, Ma'am, are you leaving so soon?"

Mineko seemed relaxed enough, and Nobee had the slightly embarrassed, annoyed expression that he always had when Sachiko saw him in the corridor of the apartment complex. Sachiko felt relieved.

"Thanks for the drink," she said. Sachiko turned her eyes away from the embracing couple and raced up the stairs. It was already dark when she got outside. She felt suddenly miserable. Shūtarō had never once looked at her with eyes that intense. He had never once enticed her to some deep place with a voice like that. Sachiko was overcome with anger at Shūtarō, who was no doubt playing mah-jongg at this very moment. Even the neon lights seemed to be mocking her.

AS USUAL, SHŪTARŌ CAME home after midnight. As soon as he got in, he drank some water and then yawned loudly several times in a row.

"Your yawns get bigger and bigger, don't they?"

"If I went and did my yawning somewhere else, that would be a bigger problem, wouldn't it?"

"The words 'marriage' and 'home,' do they mean 'a place where you yawn all the time?'"

Her husband's response was an even bigger yawn.

Sachiko turned away from Shūtarō, who was putting on his pajamas, and stood in the kitchen. She turned the faucet on all the way and stood fixed in place while the cup overflowed with water. *There are women who are rich, so rich that they overflow. And there are also empty women.*

"Ueno. Oku. Akabane. Urawa. Ōmiya. Miyahara. Ageo. Okegawa." She heard that voice again.

THE NEXT MORNING MADE the previous night's events seem like a false memory. It was as if the morning newspaper and milk chased away that muddy, guilty atmosphere. The man and woman became energetic workers. Sachiko saw Shūtarō off and started work with her sewing machine. She thought she smelled gas, but that was probably just her imagination.

Sachiko found herself stopping her work. Something was happening on the other side of the wall. A woman was moaning. She could hear a man groaning. Sachiko's own form—her body stuck to the wall like a gecko, listening—was reflected in the mirror.

"Oh, gross."

It was all the more revolting in the morning. As if to shake it off, Sachiko put on a record. She put the Bach on at a high volume. She fixed the angle of the painting hung on the wall and started sewing, but it still bothered her. She lowered the volume on the stereo. She could hear the woman's moans again. She raised the volume higher than before. She thought she could smell gas.

Sachiko walked out onto the balcony and leaned over to look into the apartment next door. The lace curtains were swaying. On the other side of the curtains, a woman's hand was trying to open the glass door, scratching the air. Sachiko could see a line of blood on the woman's wrist.

Sachiko climbed over the divider on the balcony. Mineko had collapsed on the other side of the glass door. Using a pot on the balcony that held a withered houseplant, Sachiko smashed a hole in the door. The smell of gas reached her nose.

As Sachiko screamed, "Someone! Call the building manager! Please call 911," she stuck her hand through the hole in the door and unlocked it. She was flustered and couldn't get the door open at first.

"Somebody, come over here!" Sachiko screamed as she flew into the room. A naked man lay motionless, his body partially slipping off the double bed. It was Nobee. Sachiko coughed violently as she tried to tug the unconscious Mineko outside. Fanning the gas aside with one hand, Sachiko pulled down the hem of Mineko's gown, which had been flipped up. She jumped back out onto the balcony and screamed, "Please call 911!"

SACHIKO STARED BLANKLY AT the stretchers that carried the two into an ambulance.

"They're saying it was a lovers' double suicide."

"Did they die?"

"I heard that they're still breathing."

Sachiko could hear the voices of other people in the apartment building. She realized for the first time that her wrist was bleeding. She had probably cut it on the glass door.

"SHE WAS MY NEIGHBOR, but she moved in less than three months ago. No, not me, she moved in." For the first time in her life, Sachiko had a TV microphone thrust in front of her.

"I can't really say that we're close. The most we ever really talked about was things like 'Hey, the garbage truck is late today, isn't it?' That kind of stuff—wait, are you already recording? Stop—not when I look like this." Today of all days she had a clip in her hair and was wearing a frayed blouse.

"How did you feel when you went into the room?"

"I was completely dazed. I guess that's the word,

dazed." For some reason, Sachiko was breathing heavily.

"This is the first time anything like this has ever happened to me. For me, every day is just normal. Suicide, or a double suicide, or anything like that—you never think that kind of thing could happen around you. But that's not true, is it? You can think it won't happen and then when you don't see it coming, it happens next door like a smack on the cheek. But it's not really that strange. I think it was Saikaku who wrote it, but Taruya Osan, from that book, *Five Women Who Loved Love*—oh, maybe it's Osen. Um, Osan, the wife of the man from the *koyomi*, I think that's what it's called in old Japanese, or I guess now we say 'calendar store,' and then there's what's-his-name. Oh, it's Osen from the scroll-mounting store. Osan. Shoot, I've gotten it mixed up." Sachiko laughed as she spoke, going on and on.

"Philandering, double suicide—even though they decided to do something so reckless, a totally, totally ordinary woman lived next door to them. I think she was surprised like me. Oh, the button on my shirt, it's come loose. And I sew on buttons as part of my part-time job. This is so embarrassing."

Sachiko was worked up and laughing excessively.

"My husband? He's a businessman. A completely ordinary—stop—are you still filming this?" The interview ended with Sachiko moving her hand, bandaged at the wrist, to cover the screen.

SACHIKO OPENED THE FRIDGE and was picking at some leftovers when the phone rang. A voice shouted at her with no warning: "Don't be such a disgrace!" It was Shūtarō. "The TV, I'm talking about the TV."

"You saw me on TV?"

"Someone just died and you were blabbing on and on!" His voice was shrill. "What kind of an idiot would be happily chattering away like that?"

"They're not dead! They were rescued. I saved them."

"Even if you helped them, this is still a matter of life and death. This isn't something where you get excited and chatter and laugh about it."

"I wasn't laughing!"

"Yes you were. You were laughing like some happy fool. It's offensive."

"Hello?"

"And then—don't talk about things you don't know!"

"Huh?"

"What was that about Saikaku's *Five Women*? When I heard that, I broke out in a cold sweat. You couldn't keep Osan straight from Osen, and then that crap about the calendar store."

"But I was tested on it in high school."

"If you wanted to talk about that you should have read it carefully first!"

"This isn't a normal day. I got flustered and I mixed it up."

"No matter how flustered you are, don't talk about your husband."

"What did I say?"

"'He's some ordinary businessman.' That may be true, but that's not the kind of thing you publicize on TV."

"They asked me a question, so I just answered it."

"The people in my company saw it too. I'm a laughingstock."

"It's not like I wanted to be on TV. The building manager had gone to the hospital and they pounded on the door and then stuck those microphones in my face. There was nothing I could do."

"Then you should have left the house."

"And gone where?"

"Can't you figure that much out for yourself?"

The call ended with a clang that echoed in Sachiko's ear.

He didn't even ask once if I was hurt, thought Sachiko as she left the apartment. She thought she could hear the phone ringing again when she got to the door, but she didn't go back.

At the bookstore in front of the train station, Sachiko picked up a paperback copy of Saikaku's *Five Women Who Loved Love*. Then she went to the café next door and ordered a coffee. She opened the book to the second story, "The Tale of the Amorous Barrelmaker."

> TROUBLED BY LOVE, THE MAN CLEANS A WELL
>
> Life is limited and love is not. He realized the fleeting nature of the world from the coffins he made with his own hands, making a living in the world working busily with his saw and drill. . . .

WHEN SACHIKO LIFTED THE coffee cup, her hand was still trembling. She turned to the modern language translation in the book.

"Human life is limited, but love's pathway never ends."

Her eyes followed the letters, but in her heart she heard that voice. "Asada from Hōbundō," wasn't it? When she came to herself, she got up and flipped through a phone book. In the photography and framing section there was a listing for a store called Hōbundō.

"Hello, this is Hōbundō." When Sachiko dialed

the number, she heard that voice. She hung up the phone and wrote down the address on a memo pad. It felt like her hand was moving by itself.

Hōbundō was in front of the train station, two stops away. It was a sizeable store, and inside there were two or three clerks besides Asada. Sachiko saw him smoking a cigarette while he joked around with a saleswoman. It seemed like he hadn't heard the news about Mineko.

"Um, excuse me," Sachiko spoke in a faltering, small voice. "Sir, do you know what happened to that person?"

"What person?"

"She tried to commit double suicide. She was injured. It was horrible."

Sachiko gave Asada the story in the warehouse at the back of the shop. There were messy piles of broken picture frames around them, and it smelled of glue.

"It doesn't seem like her life is in danger. She inhaled some gas too, but it doesn't sound like her injuries are too bad."

"I see."

Given that Asada didn't ask about the other man, he must have already known.

After asking Sachiko about her injured wrist, he said, "Did she tell you to come and let me know about this?"

"No, when you were making a phone call in her bar, you mentioned the name of this place."

Oh, I see, said Asada's expression.

"But even so, how'd you know that I—oh, you saw me coming and going from the apartment since you live next door—" he began to say. "No, I only went to that apartment once and I've never seen your face before."

"I could tell from your voice. I heard you make that phone call and I thought, oh, it's the same voice. 'Ueno. Oku. Akabane. Urawa. Ōmiya.'" Then Sachiko realized her error. "Oh, I'm sorry. The walls in the apartment are pretty thin, I guess. Even if you're not trying to eavesdrop, snoring, even sighs, every sound just goes right through them. Oh. . ."

This was hitting a man who was already down.

The man's every word and action had been overheard. He quietly looked to the side and put his hand on a broken picture frame. Sachiko dropped her head and nearly ran out of the store. She was furious with herself. She hadn't been asked and yet she'd gone out of her way to look up the address of Asada's store and then actually visit it. Her guilt-ridden anticipation had swelled up like a balloon and now it had popped, leaving only disappointment and misery. She was so embarrassed by the stink of her own horrible behavior that she couldn't even lift up her head.

There were footsteps chasing after her. The footsteps fell into a walking pace behind her and then Asada's voice was close to her ear.

"Please have a drink with me."

THE PLACE WAS EMPTY, maybe because it was still daytime. It wasn't quite a regular bar, but it also wasn't exactly a snack bar.

They sat side by side at the counter and Asada clinked their glasses of whiskey and water violently. Sachiko couldn't guess his feelings, but she held the glass in her bandaged hand and caught another hard clink from Asada.

He drank three whiskies without saying a word, and Sachiko had two. When they went outside, Sachiko suddenly felt the alcohol.

"Are you hungry?" Asada asked.

"Yes." Sachiko realized that she hadn't eaten much at all since the morning.

Asada bought some popcorn from a street stand, and without warning he put some in Sachiko's mouth. The two of them ate while they walked. Asada would eat some himself and put some into Sachiko's mouth. His hands, smelling of glue, touched Sachiko's lips. Each time he put popcorn into her mouth, something rose inside her. He did it again.

EVEN IN BED, ASADA's motions were rough. But there was also a strange kindness about them. Asada threw Sachiko's bandaged wrist above his head, treating it alone differently from the rest of her. Sachiko held his back with that hand and dug her nails into him. Tears flowed from the corners of her eyes. She could see the setting sun through the curtains of the love hotel.

"Please don't turn on the light."

In the darkness, Sachiko asked about techniques for making picture frames.

"Well, you can't be jealous of the pictures," said Asada. He would eliminate his own jealousy and then think about how best to show off the painting. He had wanted to be an artist but didn't have the talent. To prove as much to himself once and for all, he was going to head to New York soon.

"What if we go together?" he asked.

"You and me?"

"You've got a passport, so it should be easy."

"Ah, how do you know about that?"

"Before you were going to leave for Paris, you came down with appendicitis. You have a habit of always choking at the most important moment."

"Oh, I see. When I said that earlier." Finally, Sachiko was able to laugh. "Last year, I thought, 'I'm going to go with my friends even if it means taking on a part-time job.'"

"What's your part-time job?"

"Subcontracted sewing work. Twelve hundred yen per blouse."

SACHIKO SLIPPED OUT OF the bed to shower. As Asada tried to close Sachiko's half-open bag, he spotted a paperback inside it. It was Saikaku's *Five Women Who Loved Love*. When he paged through it, chapter four caught his eye: "The Tale of the Greengrocer and His Bundle of Love."

> A PLACE FOR A TRYST ON A SNOWY NIGHT
> In this world, we must always be on guard. There are things we must not show others: when on the road, the money stashed on your person; when drunk, your dagger; when dealing with a monk who claims to have renounced worldly pursuits, your daughter. . . .

WHILE HE MUMBLED "THE money stashed on your person, huh," Asada opened the small red purse and looked inside. Inside were three one-thousand-yen bills, precisely folded. It was touching. He took an envelope from his pocket containing three hundred thousand yen, removed three ten-thousand-yen bills, and put them in the wallet. He sensed Sachiko opening the bathroom door and put a cigarette in his mouth. Sachiko, now prepared to return home, was reflected in the glass window, twinkling with the neon lights of the love hotels all around them.

"Are you heading home?" he asked.

"Goodbye."

"That's it?"

"The memory will last a lifetime."

Sachiko bowed slightly, then picked up her bag and left.

SHŪTARŌ WAS DRINKING A beer and had the evening paper spread out before him.

"What happened to your hand?" His tone was tender. "A woman shouldn't go rushing into a situation like that. The moment you rush in could be just when a spark from the fridge causes a gas explosion."

"I see."

Avoiding Shūtarō's face, Sachiko turned the gas on under the teakettle. As she watched the flame, he stood up and came to her. He circled behind her and kissed the back of her neck. Sachiko squirmed, and just then the doorbell chimed. The building manager had come to return Sachiko's money. In the commotion that morning she had gone to the hospital with the ambulance, and she'd borrowed five thousand yen from Sachiko in case something came up.

It turned out that the ruckus had been a bit exaggerated; it looked like Mineko would be able to leave the hospital in two or three days.

"Sachiko, you look radiant. I guess when something like this happens a woman gets a rush of energy and blood flows to your head, even if you're not directly involved."

The manager smiled and left, but Sachiko felt the stiffness in her own smile. And when Sachiko put the five thousand yen into her wallet, her expression hardened again. There were three new bills she had no memory of. Asada must have put them in her wallet. Sachiko had thought they were sharing a once-in-a-lifetime love, but instead he had bought her for thirty thousand yen. Her hand quivered, and then her whole body began to tremble.

Avoiding Shūtarō's eyes, Sachiko went outside to take out the garbage. She stood holding the plastic pail in front of the wooden sign that warned not to throw out garbage on days when there was no pickup.

"What's the matter?" Shūtarō was standing there. "Stop worrying about what happened today."

He took the pail from Sachiko's hand and said, "That woman's been nothing but trouble since she moved here." He clapped her on the shoulder, said, "Let's go home," and went back into the apartment ahead of her.

TWO DAYS LATER, MINEKO came to greet Sachiko, carrying a small box of cakes. Mineko had been thin before, but now she looked truly emaciated and her skin had taken on a pallor. She lowered her head as she thanked Sachiko for all her help.

"Sachiko, if you hadn't plunged in to save me, I'd be in a square box like this." Evidently she was talking about a box for cremated ashes.

Mineko looked around Sachiko's apartment. "It's the same layout of rooms, but it seems like a whole different place. I guess having a family really changes things."

Sachiko was already feeling guilty enough, but after the word "family," she couldn't even lift her head.

"This isn't right. You have no reason to drop your head like that. I'm the one who disgraced myself. This is backwards," said Mineko.

"If you dig deep enough, you'll find one or two shameful indiscretions in every household. The feeling is mutual."

"Hearing that on a day like today is really moving." Then Mineko said that any time she stepped into the hallway the eyes of the other women in the apartment complex pierced her like arrows. Mineko's voice became intimate: "Sachiko, you're the only kind one here."

"Well, we're appendix buddies."

Mineko laughed a little at Sachiko's turn of phrase, and then said that she wanted to call in a small favor from her "appendix buddy." If she went to the bank to make a withdrawal the women would stare at her and she would be horribly embarrassed, so would Sachiko lend her twenty or thirty thousand yen for the moment? Sachiko took the bills from before out from the sewing machine drawer and handed two of them over to Mineko.

Mineko sliced the air with her hand in a gesture of thanks and said, "This is a huge help." Then she turned over the bills and examined them.

"What, are they counterfeit?" asked Sachiko.

"Strange things happen, don't they? I wonder if there's another woman in this world who has the same habits as me." Mineko stared into Sachiko's eyes and spoke in a low voice. "See, when I give some money to a man I love—money I make by flattering men and pouring sake for them—rather than say any parting words, I mark the edges of the bills with lipstick like this. That's how I say goodbye."

Indeed, there was some red on the edges of the bills.

"These bills look exactly the ones I gave to a man just recently. Sachiko, where did you get this money, and from whom?"

"From whom? Any money I have must have come from my husband's work or my part-time job."

Sachiko told herself to calm down, but her voice was shrill.

"That's it?"

"What do you mean, 'That's it?' What else could there be?"

Mineko stared at Sachiko's face and let out a small laugh.

"Sorry to have bothered you." She closed the door and left.

Sachiko looked again at the red marks on the corners of the two bills, which Mineko hadn't taken, and then dropped right down to sit on the floor. She could hear voices in the hallway. It sounded like the other women in the apartment complex were ganging up on Mineko.

"I apologize for any small amount of trouble I've caused you. It's not like I've stolen any of your things, and if I fix the broken window then I don't think there's any reason I should have to leave the apartment complex." Familiar women's voices flew at Mineko in response. It sounded like three or four housewives had surrounded her.

"Wherever we go, people mention this incident. 'Oh, you're from *that* apartment building.'"

"People are saying that we're all a mess."

"A mess?" Mineko had raised her voice. "Housewives today are much more of a mess than I am! I've heard of a lot of wives who sell their bodies to men for money."

"Oh, I've heard a lot about housewife prostitution too, sure." The building manager had stepped in, probably to help Mineko, who was outnumbered by the many other women.

Sachiko, holding the three bills marked in crimson, froze and was unable to move.

ASADA HAD ALREADY LEFT for New York when Sachiko visited Hōbundō. The aging shopkeeper said that Asada had asked for a month's leave, but his guess was there was only a fifty-fifty chance Asada would come back. He handed Sachiko a note with the address of the place Asada would be staying at, a friend's studio. The man didn't ask for Sachiko's name or her relationship to Asada.

That night, as Sachiko was thinking about the bills in her sewing drawer with the red marks on their edges, Shūtarō's hands reached toward her, but she didn't want to make love. She resisted him intensely in the darkness, rose gradually from the bed, and then moved to crouch under the sewing machine.

"I'm exhausted. Sorry."

"You need to quit your part-time job."

Shūtarō rolled over and turned his back to her. *I've still got a good reason for cheating on him*, thought Sachiko. The only thing she felt guilty about was that she'd ended up basically selling herself for money.

The next day Sachiko still couldn't calm down. It felt like all the other housewives suddenly stopped their whispering when Sachiko went into the hallway. Had Mineko been telling them stories about her? Wouldn't the rumors reach Shūtarō sooner or later? When Sachiko went shopping and took out one of the ten-thousand-yen bills, it felt like everybody was staring at her. Her hands trembled.

I can't keep going on like this, she thought. She withdrew the time deposits she had saved from her part-time job and went to a travel agency. She got a visa and bought a plane ticket to New York. In the end, she had become stigmatized as a housewife whore. She had to exchange that stigma for love.

Sachiko left a note on the dinner table: "I've gone to climb Mt. Tanigawa."

She went to Narita Airport and boarded the plane. She felt possessed.

> There is absolutely no way to keep this a secret. From here on, I will abandon myself to this, make my name in it as long as I draw breath, and go with Moemon on the road to death.

PERHAPS IT WAS THE vibration from takeoff, or perhaps it was her tremulous emotional state, but Sachiko couldn't stop shaking as her eyes ran over the same words again and again in the *Five Women* paperback resting on her lap.

Sachiko could see herself, a young wife wearing traditional wedding makeup, holding hands with the sales clerk Asada, the two of them walking down the road together.

ONCE THE PLANE HAD lifted off, Sachiko's complete desperation, or maybe some newfound courage, allowed her to sleep well. She slept as if to make up for the past ten days, and she made short work of the in-flight meal. Even though this was her first trip to a foreign country, even though she was going to New York, Sachiko didn't panic. Perhaps it was because she'd become familiar with the area through TV shows or a guidebook. Compared with the particular situation she was about to encounter, stepping onto foreign soil seemed like nothing out of the ordinary.

She soon found the place where Asada was staying, on 28th Street. He was living on the sixth floor of a dilapidated seven-story building, and the elevator wasn't working. Sachiko climbed up the stairwell, dark even in the daytime, and knocked on the door. A young American man holding a cat opened it.

"Mister Asada—" she didn't know what to say after that and froze in panic. Just then, holding another cat with the same pattern in its fur, Asada peeked out from behind the American. He saw Sachiko and without saying anything let go of the cat he had been holding.

"You don't seem that surprised."

"I'm the type that doesn't look surprised even when I am." He looked Sachiko up and down as she stood there holding her suitcase, which contained only a change of clothes.

"Did you come with anyone?" he asked.

"By myself."

"What did you say when you left?"

"I said, 'I've gone to climb Mt. Tanigawa.'"

Asada laughed loudly.

"I've, um, got something that I have to give back to you." Sachiko began looking around in her bag, but Asada abruptly snatched her suitcase from her in a way that told her to be quiet.

"What do you want to see first?"

"Fifth Avenue. Times Square. Harlem. Tiffany. Carnegie Hall. The Village. SoHo. Central Park. The Dakota House." They weren't train stops, but this time it was Sachiko's turn to list off the names.

Like lovers, they held hands, swung their arms together, and enjoyed themselves as they walked around and looked at the city. Old neighborhoods and new neighborhoods. White faces and black faces passed them in the street. The words appeared stacked on top of one another: "New York," "Love," and "Elope." Sachiko had thoroughly intoxicated herself.

She drank American beer, Budweiser, smoked half of Asada's cigarettes, and listened to jazz shoulder-to-shoulder with black couples at a small bar in the Village. Her intoxication continued; in Asada's bed she was even more intoxicated, and, intoxicated, she fell asleep.

"I'm thirsty. Thirsty . . ." Sachiko was mumbling, half asleep.

She was so tired that her eyes wouldn't open.

"I'm just going to get a glass of water." As she got out of bed, she stepped on Shūtarō, or so she thought.

"I'm sorry. Oof." As she staggered around, thinking she had made her way into the kitchen where she could get some water, Sachiko collided with a partition screen. It fell noisily and broke a flowerpot.

Asada was awake now. "I wanted to get some water—in my house, this is where the kitchen is," Sachiko said, intending to laugh as she spoke.

The room grew light and then dark in turn as the neon lights outside flashed on and off. It was a loft, a warehouse space that had been remodeled into a modern apartment. A number of bicycles hung as decorations from the snow-white, gym-like ceiling. The American, woken by the noise, had come over with a cat in his arms, but to Sachiko he seemed like a huge ogre against the white wall. At his feet was the flowerpot, split wide open.

"I'm really awful. I mistook this for my apartment." Sachiko let out a big laugh, but in her nervousness it turned into something else. She suddenly dashed to her suitcase.

"Going home. I'm going home."

"Don't talk nonsense. This is New York. We're fifteen thousand kilometers from Japan."

"I'm going back. I'm going home."

"How? By foot?"

"I don't know what to do. I've done a terrible thing."

As Sachiko sobbed, "I'm scared, I'm scared," Asada held her and urged her to come back to bed. With her fear, her intoxication worsened.

"This is your punishment as an adulteress!" The gates to a dilapidated *jizō* temple opened, and in her dream Sachiko saw herself beheaded by Shūtarō, dressed as a samurai.

Sachiko moved to indulge herself with Asada.

WHEN SHE SAW THE Statue of Liberty in real life for the first time, its expression was more severe than she had expected.

"What's she holding?" asked Sachiko.

"In her right hand, a torch. In her left, the Declaration of Independence, maybe."

"Liberty and independence . . ."

"Women like those words, don't they?"

"Because we don't have them. When we get married they both just disappear. We shouldn't fall in love. Love is a crime too. In the old times women would have been killed. When married women fell in love they knew that it might lead to their death." Sachiko was becoming tense again as she spoke.

She envisioned herself and Asada in the Hudson River after their double suicide, bodies catching on the thousand wooden support beams of the piers, one rock for each of them in the riverbed, and each rock engraved with the words, "A faithful believer in Amida Buddha."

There was an abandoned highway right next to some buildings in Manhattan. It was sunset, and their two silhouettes looked like crucifixes or grave markers. Sachiko needed a drink.

SACHIKO WOKE UP AGAIN in the early morning of the third day. She thought she could hear the sound of a sewing machine.

"Hey, is there a sewing factory upstairs?"

"No, it's a sculptor's studio."

With his eyes closed, Asada held Sachiko's shoulders gently. His body looked thin when clothed, but he wasn't actually that slim. Sachiko rose from the bed and left his body, the body that had given her the satisfying intoxication Shūtarō never had.

"I can hear a sewing machine."

"You're imagining things." Asada turned his face into the bed.

Sachiko took the money from her bag and put it in the pocket of Asada's business suit. She would go home. Saikaku's women were killed, but a modern woman could start all over again.

There was hot breath on the nape of her neck. Asada, who Sachiko had thought was still in bed, was now standing up.

"I came here to give you back this money. I really don't like to borrow money for no reason, so . . ."

"Then why didn't you just give it back when you first got here? What do you mean by giving it back after you've had your fun with me and we've walked all over New York together?"

"The money was my excuse. I fell in love with you—it's okay to do it once in my lifetime. I wanted to see what it was like to fall in love."

"You're going to call it quits just like that, after

three days of this once-in-a-lifetime love? You've found a nice stopping point and now you're cutting this short to go home and pretend like nothing happened. How nice for you." Asada was as angry as he was in love with her.

"You were lying when you said you're not the type to show emotion. Your expression is scary."

"What if I say I won't let you go back?"

"I'll go home."

"What'll you say when you get back?"

"Nothing. I won't say a word and I'll sew as best I can."

Asada looked at Sachiko's desperate eyes and said just two words: "You're strong." He offered his hand as if to say, *Do your best.*

"Thank you."

No matter how long I live, I'll probably never again grip a man's hand this tightly, thought Sachiko.

IT WAS AFTER ELEVEN o'clock at night when Shūtarō walked into Puzzle.

"I'm Shūtarō Tokizawa from next door." He had already had a few drinks. He sat at the counter and greeted Mineko. She bowed silently and began making the whiskey and water that he ordered.

"Did my wife say anything to you?" Shūtarō played with the Rubik's Cube on the counter. "She's been out for a bit, and all she left was a note saying she's gone to climb Mt. Tanigawa."

"Mt. Tanigawa?" Mineko stopped chipping the ice.

"Until now she'd never even said the phrase 'mountain climbing,' but all of a sudden she runs off to Mt. Tanigawa. I don't have any idea why. If you've heard anything . . ."

Mineko's hand had frozen as she gripped the ice pick.

"Who did she go with? I doubt that's a mountain you can climb by yourself. Mt. Tanigawa, that is." Mineko's eyes stared into space.

"Well, I guess she also asked me once if I could name the train stops from Ueno to Tanigawa."

Mineko laughed. She laughed violently.

"I can't believe how rude you are," said Shūtarō. "I told you we live next door to you, and you haven't said even one word of apology for what happened a few days ago." His voice took on the force of the resentment that had built up in him over the past five days: It was his wife whose hand was injured. He wasn't demanding gratitude, but he and his wife were victims. And to top it all off, rather than apologizing, Mineko refused to respond to his questions and just laughed.

"I'm laughing because it's funny." Mineko let out another loud laugh. Then she said that she was the victim and Shūtarō's wife the perpetrator.

"Right now your wife is climbing Mt. Tanigawa all right." Mineko gulped down a straight whiskey. "But Mt. Tanigawa's not a mountain. It's a man." She said it forcefully.

"A man."

Mineko poured another whiskey and water for Shūtarō, who was dumbstruck.

"It's true. The man I loved."

"Don't be ridiculous. Sachiko couldn't manage something that slick. She's set in her ways, and she's more interested in saving some cash than seducing men." Gradually his voice grew softer. "The man, is his name Tanigawa?"

Mineko downed another drink.

"No, that's not his name. He came to my place and while he was holding me, he said, 'Ueno. Oku. Akabane. Urawa. Ōmiya,' and your wife heard it. Sure, it's bad of me to be having men over in the afternoon, but she's the one who put her ear to the wall and eavesdropped on us. She's just as guilty as me. Also, your wife—"

In her agitation Mineko had started to say, "men give her money," but she realized that this was dangerous ground.

"Men give her what?"

"Gi—give her no attention."

"She has a husband."

"Husbands aren't men." After Mineko said it, she muttered, "Oh, word games are difficult," but Shūtarō didn't seem to understand her.

"My guess is she was isolated from men so that's why she was so instantly taken with the man I brought home."

Just as Shūtarō started to say something, a drunken customer came in. Mineko said that they were closing, but the customer demanded to be let in to the bar.

"Go home!" shouted Shūtarō in a startlingly loud voice. His hand shook as he held his glass. Mineko poured more alcohol into that glass. She also poured some for herself.

"You've been married for?"

"Seven years."

"If you work in the nightlife business for seven years you learn how things work, but I guess with marriage, seven years isn't enough."

SHŪTARŌ AND MINEKO WERE tangled together as they climbed the outdoor staircase of the apartment building. Mineko stood next to him as he swayed and tried to unlock the door to his apartment. She put her hand over the keyhole. The door to her apartment was half open, her eyes inviting Shūtarō inside.

"The layout of the rooms is the same, isn't it?" he asked.

"That's right. The same layout." Taking off his dress shirt, she pulled Shūtarō's hands to her body. "Women also have the same layout, you know."

She pushed Shūtarō down onto the bed, and said, "What do you think? It's the same, isn't it?"

Shūtarō's hands unfastened the buttons on her dress.

Mineko opened her eyes and whispered, "I can always hear you. When you do this. The sound of the sewing machine, coming from the other side of the wall: *kata-kata-kata*. It used to make me feel relieved when I heard it. Because then I couldn't hear your voices. But gradually it started to bother me. 'I'm a married woman. Our names have been properly entered into the national family register and we're recognized by society.' To me, that's what it was saying. 'What are you? You're not a proper woman.' No matter how many boyfriends I take up with, it's like catching sand in a sieve. I'm left with absolutely nothing. Sewing and making blouses for a part-time job, that leaves you with a good home."

"So is this your revenge?"

"That's right. My revenge." Mineko had pressed herself against him, but was suddenly left unsupported when Shūtarō propped himself up.

"Isn't that the sewing machine?"

"You're imagining it. I can't hear anything. For one thing, if she were home she'd have the light on."

Shūtarō had started to make love to Mineko but was now just going through the motions. She climbed out of the bed and handed him his dress shirt, which had fallen on the floor.

"I guess you don't have the courage."

Shūtarō silently buttoned his shirt.

"Or maybe I'm wrong. Maybe it takes more courage to go home."

"I'd like to believe that."

Shūtarō even knotted his tie carefully. Perhaps that was just his personality.

"This is marriage," he sneered at himself.

"You have no freedom." Mineko laughed too, but her speech was shaky. "It's pretty great, actually. Though it makes me feel terrible." Mineko's eyes were wet and shining.

She opened the door and saw him out with a "good night."

"Good night," said Shūtarō.

Soon, she heard the neighboring door open and close.

THE APARTMENT BUILDING HAD put up a Japanese flag for some national holiday.

Sachiko came home carrying her suitcase. She stopped and stood at the bottom of the apartment staircase, calmed her breathing, and then climbed all the stairs without stopping. She was used to climbing these stairs but now they seemed higher and steeper than usual. She had to climb them to get home.

Shūtarō was sleeping in his perpetually unmade bed next to a mountain of empty beer cans.

Sachiko called out, "I'm home!" Her voice was loud and cheerful.

Shūtarō, eyes shut, said nothing.

Sachiko shouted it again. She was frantic. This time her tone was even more cheerful, her voice even louder. "I'm home!"

"Welcome home." Shūtarō said it with his eyes closed. "How was Tanigawa?"

"Well, I didn't actually go to climb Mt. Tanigawa."

"Shut up!" Shūtarō quickly followed that with a softer, "Be quiet."

"In fact," he said, "I went to the foot of a mountain too."

"The foot of a mountain . . ."

"I was told that coming back home would be braver than climbing it."

"Who told you that?"

Shūtarō opened his eyes. His stubbly face, eyes crusted with sleep, was a strangely welcome sight for Sachiko.

"Let's talk about it when we're seventy or eighty."

"Sure." Sachiko swallowed a big lump in her throat. "From now on, I'm going to keep it together."

"Do that for me," he said.

Shūtarō got up and hit Sachiko's sturdy behind once with a *smack*. Sachiko turned away, covered her face with both hands, and began to sob.

"Which of us are you crying about?" asked Shūtarō. Sachiko sobbed loudly into his chest like a child.

MINEKO MOVED OUT JUST three days later. She skipped out on two months' rent and didn't pay Sachiko back for the dry cleaning and gas bills—it might as well have been an escape in the night.

Aside from the whiskey, soda bottles, and old newspapers left in front of her door and the bare double bed left in her room, everything else had disappeared entirely.

THE RAINY SEASON HAD just ended. Sachiko, carrying a big parcel wrapped in cloth, was taking her usual bumpy bus ride. Inside the parcel were materials for her part-time job. Collars, sleeves, bodices. Sachiko made the blouses by sewing these separated parts of a woman's body back together.

Almost a month had passed since she had returned to her life as the solitary housewife Sachiko Tokizawa. She was the only one who understood the scars from that experience. Now, she prepared food and sewed just a bit more carefully than she had before.

While the bus was stopped at a traffic light, Sachiko looked out the window at the road next to the bus and gasped. Down below she could see Mineko, riding behind a man on a motorcycle, with her hands on his waist, laughing.

Sachiko felt like she had met someone she had yearned terribly to see. She wanted to call out to Mineko. She wanted to say something. But the light turned green, the two vehicles parted quickly, and soon they were far away.

Happiness

SUMMER WEDDING DRESSES ARE exasperating work for a seamstress. If there are any sweat stains on the fabric, she'll have to reimburse the buyer. And because the cloth is pure white, it's forbidden for even a leaf beetle, drawn to the light, to touch the fabric.

Motoko continued blind stitching the hem of the dress as she wiped the sweat from her forehead and neck with a cool towel. At twenty-seven, she had been employed as a seamstress for some time, working earnestly for the same Western-style dressmaker. Her income wasn't at the same level as that of an office assistant at a top company, but she had gained skill and her salary had increased accordingly. It wouldn't be hard for her to install an air conditioner, and yet she wouldn't buy one. *If I had an air conditioner, I'd never leave the house*, she kept telling herself. She'd become set in her ways, and anyway if things went well Motoko's guess was that her own love life would be progressing nicely just around the time when the cool autumn breezes started to blow.

Motoko could sew other people's wedding clothes cheerfully because she had a lover of her own. That hadn't been true last summer. Sewing a long dress for a woman working in the nightlife business never bothered her, but she had become exasperated working on a bridal gown.

"WHILE MEN PICK OUT wives, and women pick out husbands, I sit in the sun and pick out lice."

Thinking about it, Motoko had realized that the technique with which she textured the fabric, scooping the needle down and then up, one stitch at a time, was the same technique that the old folks in the countryside had taught Motoko and the other kids her age as they sang to them about "picking out lice." She and the other kids hadn't even know what lice were. Angry with herself for remembering the song, Motoko had then done something absolutely forbidden.

She had wiped her armpits with a cool towel and then tried on the bridal dress that she had just finished sewing. Trying it on didn't do anything for her, and in the mirror she saw a dark face aged beyond its years. Motoko had made sure there was no smell or yellow tint and delivered the garment, but when the dressmaker inspected it, she put her nose close to the armpits of the dress. The dressmaker said nothing, but Motoko burned with humiliation.

Motoko had a slight body odor. It was the reason she had abandoned her dream of becoming a beautician without even trying to land a job and had instead chosen dressmaking, which she could do from home.

THE TV NEXT DOOR was rattling off the seven o'clock news. Just when Motoko had found a good stopping point, put down her needle, and was getting up to have dinner, the manager of the apartment building knocked on her door. There was a phone call from Izu with a message that Motoko's father had collapsed. He was nearly seventy years old.

Carrying a travel bag into which she had thrown

only a change of underwear, Motoko ran through a shortcut behind a factory. The neighborhoods from Ōmori to Kamata in Tokyo were full of huge factories, and the little workshops in this area looked forlorn.

And yet, although the workshops appeared dilapidated and dead at first glance, the smell of machine oil and burning chips was proof that they were alive. The chips were waste from the steel that was shaved and processed on lathes and milling machines. It may have been high tide, because the Ebitori and Nomi rivers, which flow into the sea around Tokyo's Haneda Airport, carried a nasty smell of the sea mixed with garbage, and the odors drifted brazenly in the darkness.

The surface of the dark water moved viscously, like coal tar, and the sparse lights flickered on the water in reflection. Most of the small factories had closed their shutters, but slivers of light and sound leaked out from the shops where people were working overtime. These factories did subcontract work for the big, increasingly automated factories, as well as some sample product manufacturing, and business wasn't bad.

Noguchi Ironworks had its lights on as well.

It was a small workshop, a renovated former residence, with just one employee besides the owner. Kazuo worked there as the lathe operator. Just now he had finished his night shift and was wiping his oil-stained hands with an old newspaper. He was clearly bewildered by the sight of Motoko running up to him, gasping for breath.

"My dad is already pretty old, and I want to you to meet him while he's still around."

Kazuo had always been a man of few words, and

now, apparently surprised at the suddenness of this, he simply exchanged his old newspaper for a dirty rag and wiped his hands silently.

"You won't?"

"I'm not saying that, but . . ."

"It's only been a month and now she's dragging me off to see her father, right? You must think I'm really taking advantage."

"No, that's not it."

"Your clothes are fine as is. Please."

Now she just had to gaze unflinchingly into Kazuo's eyes—he was a head taller than she was—and wait patiently.

Her father was at death's door, but she was all worked up about dragging this man into the situation. Kazuo had just turned thirty and lived with his sister, who was much younger. He slowly changed his clothes like a man who couldn't decide what he was going to do, but that was how he always was. He didn't say things clearly; he was careless about both money and time. Maybe even life. He worked slowly and impassively, like a grazing cow. And he made love to Motoko like a cow chewing cud.

He had failed his college entrance examinations, and what was apparently supposed to be a short stay at a small factory in town had dragged on. He remained there but had no hopes for the future. Twenty years ago, her father surely would have asked if this man had any redeeming characteristics at all, but these days she didn't expect her father to say something like that. And if he did, Motoko knew how she would respond: "We don't need a reason to fall in love. That goes for you too, doesn't it?"

Yūzō, her father, was living with a woman in a tourist area of Izu that had gone downhill.

"Don't be surprised, okay? The woman he's living with is really young," Motoko warned Kazuo. But the woman her father was living with, Tae, was probably two or three years past forty. She ran a luggage-checking business; he had met her when he went on a fishing trip to Izu ten years earlier and, discarding his wife and children, he had moved to Izu for good.

While her mother was alive, Motoko had held a grudge against her father, and she had believed she would never forgive him. But her mother died, and after hearing that her father had high blood pressure, Motoko had started showing up to join him for the New Year's holiday two or three years ago.

IT WAS QUITE LATE when they arrived at Izu. The train station had been ignored by commercial developers, and there weren't even any touts for traditional Japanese inns. Beetles swarmed around the weak lights.

Yūzō's—no, Tae's—store was just a short walk from the train station, on an old thoroughfare next to the sea.

WE RENT FISHING RODS.

When she saw those proper, precise characters, written in a bold hand on a piece of wood, Motoko said, "That's my father's writing."

As she pointed out the sign to Kazuo, who was standing behind her, Motoko suddenly thought that if her father died she'd take the sign with her as a memento. But then, frantically rejecting those thoughts, she pulled aside the stained curtain and knocked on the glass door behind it.

"It's Motoko. Motoko from Tokyo."

Even Motoko was surprised by the desperation in

her own voice. While she was en route this had felt like her first trip with her boyfriend, but now she suddenly felt guilty.

Yūzō, however, was sitting on his futon and watching TV with the same healthy face Motoko had seen at the last New Year's holiday.

"Dad, is it okay for you to be up?"

Motoko entered the room and when Yūzō saw her he looked away, appearing startled. He was always like that.

"At one point I thought things might go south, but. . ." said Tae, whose face, body, and even voice were round. She smiled airily as she glanced intermittently at Kazuo.

"What on earth happened?"

"A student came by. From a long time ago."

"A student?"

"A customer came in to check some luggage and then exclaimed, 'Oh! Mr. Principal!'"

"What did Dad do?"

"He was sweating a lot. He asked what year and what class the student was—I say student, but this guy was middle-aged, almost forty."

Yūzō had worked his way intently through the field of education and his last position had been principal of a junior high school. As soon as he reached the mandatory retirement age and left his job, he underwent a great change, perhaps in reaction to the severity and strictness he had always applied to his own life. In his old age, he let go of all his principles at once.

Gesticulating and mimicking Yūzō's tone of voice, Tae said, "You take care of yourself. I'll do the same." She waved her hand just like the emperor and said, "Then, the minute the customer left—"

and then she rolled back her eyes and purposely fell against Kazuo. Perhaps she felt bad for Kazuo, who hadn't been introduced and was in an awkward position.

Motoko asked if the fall could have simply been caused by dizziness.

"Thinking about it now, that was probably it," said Tae. "But I really feel responsible for him and he's so important to me, you know? What if the worst happens?"

She laughed again in Kazuo's direction.

"Sensei." Tae had been using that name for Yūzō for a long time.

"Sensei, say hello. Motoko, this is your husband, right?"

"We're not that far along yet."

"She came to introduce him to you. Look, Sensei."

Yūzō's body was so desiccated that it looked like he was going to snap, but his solid build and good posture from his days as a principal hadn't changed. Maybe because he felt embarrassed, he always played dumb for the first hour or so.

Just as Motoko started to introduce Kazuo there was a knock at the door and an "Excuse me." It was a slightly husky woman's voice. Her sister Kumiko had finally arrived.

"LITTLE SIS."

Tae was getting up to greet Kumiko but Motoko stood as if to push Tae aside.

"I missed the train. I took a taxi from Atami."

"That must have been expensive! All the way from Atami."

"Forget that—how's Dad?"

Motoko related the incident of their father being called Mr. Principal by a customer who came to drop off some luggage. “It’s his punishment,” laughed Kumiko in relief.

Tae then came to the door. “Thank you for all your help,” said Kumiko. Her voice didn’t sound forced and she bowed to Tae. But as she started to move inside she saw Kazuo and muttered icily, “What’s Kazuo doing here?”

Perhaps not hearing Kumiko’s comment, Tae introduced them in a relaxed tone. She started to say, “This is Motoko’s husband” but then added, “Well, I guess not yet.” Tae looked at Kumiko’s and then Kazuo’s stiff expressions, and then at Motoko. She swallowed her words.

“So you know each other. You’ve met before, I guess.”

There was silence, though it lasted barely a moment. Maybe because of the moisture of the sea, or poor ventilation, or because of the haphazard piles of junk that Tae seemed to have forgotten to throw out, the low-ceilinged, six-tatami-mat living room was filled with the stale, tobacco-heavy stench of an old man.

Motoko, the smallish younger sister with plain features, was the exact opposite of her older sister, who was tall and stylish. If the younger sister sat formally and wrote in print, the older sister would sit at ease and write in flowing cursive. Kumiko didn’t use any exceptional makeup but nonetheless had a glow about her. This was perhaps because these past ten years she had been working in the nightlife business, having moved into it after working at a coffee shop.

Kumiko looked at her little sister and let out a

small laugh. "The one I know is actually this guy's older brother."

Addressing Tae, she explained, "Ten years ago his brother dumped me."

Motoko looked at Kazuo, trying to catch even the slightest change in his expression. It was fair to say that she had pulled Kazuo out here because she wanted to see these two together in this moment. Compared to Kumiko's shocked reaction, Kazuo's facial expression hadn't changed much.

"How's your brother doing?" Although Kumiko's voice was suddenly cheerful, her tone had a perceptible bite to it.

"I haven't seen him in a long time, but he's probably fine."

"But he's your brother! You should know more than that. But I guess that's just the way it is. We're like that too."

Then Kumiko turned to Motoko and asked how long she and Kazuo had been together.

Motoko answered that it was a pretty recent relationship and asked, "Are you surprised?" She looked into her sister's eyes.

"Why would I be surprised?"

Yūzō's curiosity was obvious as he stared intently at the three of them. Suddenly, he leapt at Kazuo and punched him. He hit Kazuo two or three more times with remarkable speed for an old man. Kazuo was bewildered and didn't defend himself, and Yūzō pushed aside the three startled women who tried to stop him.

"Don't stop me. This bastard—" yelled Yūzō, wheezing as he shook off the women who had piled up on him to block him. "You ruined my daughter's life! And so shamelessly!"

Kumiko stepped in and broke it up. "Dad, you've got it wrong. This man is his little brother."

"Huh?"

"You're thinking of Taichirō. He's the older brother."

"So it's the older brother."

"Yes. That was the older brother. This is the younger brother. Why are you hitting the younger brother?"

"What? So, he's the one who said he would marry you then at the last minute dumped you and married some girl from a rich family?"

"That was this man's older brother. Dad, you've got it wrong." Yūzō was becoming even more vehement, but Kumiko said to him in a low voice, "Let's stop talking about the past. There are stories I don't want anyone to bring up again."

Now told that he was attacking the younger brother instead of the older one, Yūzō suddenly put his head in his hands and squatted down. As Yūzō groaned, "It hurts! My head hurts," the younger sister was harder-hearted than the older one.

"Dad, there's no reason for you to have a headache. Kazuo's the one in pain."

There was a mysterious thread of connection among the three of them. Tae stared at them in silence, perhaps guessing as much. Even Motoko didn't really know what kind of expressions they would be wearing or what kind of conversation they would be having if Yūzō hadn't sprung up and punched Kazuo.

AFTER HANDING OVER THE only mosquito net in the house to the three visitors, Yūzō and Tae retreated to the adjacent room, which was four and a half tatami mats in size. In fact, it was the only other room in the house.

There were no extra pillows, so Tae wrapped a towel around a floor cushion for each of them. While doing so, she whispered that it was time for a TV show instructing women how to put on kimonos and that Yūzō was hooked on this show these days.

"It's like Japanese-style reverse-stripping, don't you think?"

Yūzō appeared to have no interest in probing into any hard feelings between his daughters. He fixed his eyes, which were nearly the color of water, on the sky and fanned himself comfortably on the edge of the veranda.

Kazuo slipped under the mosquito net first, lying down at its very edge. The lamps were dimmed and in the faint light Kumiko was changing into a cotton kimono she had borrowed from Tae to use as pajamas. Just ahead of her, Motoko moved under the mosquito net still wearing her white slip and lay down next to Kazuo. Outside the net, Kumiko's hands froze as she was tying the dark crimson under-sash of her robe. But just a moment later, there was again the sound of the sash like a snake slithering along a stone wall. The light went out, and Kumiko entered the net holding a fan. Something told Motoko that the three of them, lined up side by side, were breathing harder than usual.

"I wonder why she called us. This wasn't a big deal," said Kumiko quietly.

Motoko was bothered by the smoke from the mosquito-repellent incense in the next room, which had its door slightly ajar. In her usual small voice, she said, "Maybe she wanted to show us how she's taking such good care of him." That was Motoko's only answer, and after that there was just darkness and the breathing of three bodies.

There was no hint of wind from the sea or the mountains, and the three of them became soaked with sweat. Motoko could feel her mouth getting dry, a warning that she was beginning to tense up, physically and mentally. *It's not as bad as you think*, Motoko's late mother had said, but that—that smell—this kind of situation was exactly when it would emanate from her armpits. Motoko groped for Kazuo's hand as he lay next to her.

Kumiko, do you remember that time?

It was the summer before Motoko's senior year of high school. The night when she and Kumiko had talked while lying side by side under a mosquito net, just like they were now. When Motoko said, *I'm going to become a beautician. After I graduate from high school, I want to go to beauty school.*

Kumiko had objected. "You're not cut out for that."

Motoko wouldn't drop it. She kept asking why.

"You know why. I don't need to say it," Kumiko had muttered.

Was Kumiko talking about *that*? *That,* the last thing that Motoko wanted anyone to bring up? At that point Motoko had sensed her body getting hot.

Kumiko apparently took her sister's lack of response as a lack of understanding. "I guess you don't understand because you haven't been to a beauty parlor yet, but when a beautician gives shampoos and haircuts, her armpits move right around the customer's face. You should pick another job. Only a sister could say this to you, so you should be thankful."

Kumiko always used that phrasing when she said something unpleasant. Her wording was deliberately rough and insensitive; she would plunge the dagger all the way in, and then she and her victim would be in an all-out battle. Motoko had a sense of this even as a child, and if she had had a knife at that moment she surely would have stabbed her sister in the chest.

But, Kumiko.

You don't need to worry about me any more.

Right now, this instant, sure my body smells, but isn't there a stronger smell?

Kazuo's fingers.

The nape of Kazuo's neck.

And Kazuo's armpits.

Machine oil has seeped into them. Don't you smell it?

From the top of his head to the tips of his toes. That's right. People who work with lathes and milling machines have to wear solid, bulky safety shoes that protect them from falling tools, and somehow the oil even seeps into those too. Even the spaces under his toenails smell like machine oil.

Motoko entangled her feet with Kazuo's.

The first time we were together, Kazuo said simply, "I smell. A woman mentioned it when I went to a cabaret show once. She said, 'You smell just like my father. I noticed it as soon as you sat down.'"

"No wonder I'm not popular with women," Kazuo muttered to me. But I turned the tables on him right then; I put my sweaty right armpit up to his face.

While I held my armpit there, I stared at his facial expression, his body, everything. He inhaled deeply. He inhaled that smell from my body. If I felt like he was put off by it, even a tiny bit, if I felt like he was forcing himself to tolerate it, I was going to jump to my feet and go home. I wouldn't have seen him again after that.

But, Kumiko.

Kazuo, he exhaled quietly and calmly, and inhaled deeply one more time. I thought he looked like a little boy smelling flowers for the first time. I want to show you that face. The moment I thought of showing it to you, my neck arched back and the tips of my blood vessels all turned to hot water at once, and then I could barely move.

Not to quote you, but this is one of those times when one could say, "You know why. I don't need to say it."

Kumiko was breathing as if asleep.

You're not sleeping, are you? It's stifling in here, so you must be faking it.

Motoko wanted to shake Kumiko awake and ask her one more thing.

Your relationship with Kazuo is that he's the little brother of the man who dumped you. You're the woman his older brother dumped. But is that all there is to it? Am I just imagining that there's an invisible thread stretched between you two?

Then Motoko heard Tae's voice: "You're doing it again!"

"How many times do I have to tell you?" Tae was clearly reprimanding someone in the darkness. Her voice was coming from the storefront portion of the building.

Yūzō, his robe open in the front, had opened a travel bag that one of the customers had dropped off. Tae had stopped him as he was pulling out its contents.

"I told you, you can't open the luggage that people check with us."

"I'm not going to steal anything."

"You still can't do it even if you don't steal anything. This business is what keeps food on our table. No one's going to check their luggage here if people start saying that we secretly look into people's bags."

"What if there's a bomb in here?"

"There's nothing of the sort. Sensei, come on, go to sleep now."

The sounds of the futon being pulled back were accompanied by constant, phlegmy coughing, and soon it was quiet.

When he was a principal, their father had hated any kind of impropriety, to a fault. Once, during either the New Year or midyear holidays, a couple of parents had come by the house with a gift certificate for Yūzō. Motoko's mother inadvertently accepted it because the parents had handed it over together with the customary box of sweets. Yūzō came home late that night but shouted at his wife to take the gift back at once. Motoko remembered seeing her mother change into a kimono late that night and leave the house.

That same Yūzō was now looking into other people's luggage. And judging from Tae's remarks, this was apparently a regular occurrence.

What on earth was her seventy-year-old father looking at? What was he hoping to see?

Kumiko's elbow hit Motoko.

Motoko wondered if Kumiko wanted to say something and turned toward her. Kumiko, her eyes full of tears, smiled at Motoko.

"Kumiko." Motoko realized that her own voice was now the same as it had been when she was a child. Motoko's hand was no longer gripping Kazuo's.

MOTOKO SENSED THAT SHE had been beset by unsettling dreams, perhaps because she wasn't sleeping on her usual pillow. But the dreams vanished as soon as she opened her eyes, leaving behind a messy listlessness.

Why are dreams in the summer so especially tiring? Even in the dreamworld, summer is still summer.

Motoko groped for Kazuo next to her. He wasn't there. Reflexively, she searched for Kumiko on her other side. Kumiko turned over and let out a low groan.

Kazuo was sitting on the open veranda, smoking and looking out at the so-called "garden." It was really a garden in name only, just a small piece of vacant land. Apparently Tae's store not only checked luggage but also sold beer and soda; empty cases had been thrown into the yard and were now covered in white dust. There were also a rotting weather-beaten straw hat and crushed, empty drink cans that had probably been flung into the yard from the road. Here and there among the scattered trash, morning glories, wild basil plants, and frail stalks of corn had been painstakingly planted.

The smell of cigarette smoke wafted through the darkness. Motoko felt incredibly peaceful. She wanted to think that this was how she and Kazuo would be living years from now. The wife was sleeping. Late at night, the husband was smoking alone in the darkness on the veranda by the bed. Half-dreaming, she smelled his usual cigarette smoke and then dozed off again. When she woke in the morning, she would forget that too.

Motoko thought she could remember a similar scene from her childhood one time when she had gotten up to use the bathroom, but maybe she was misremembering it. No, it definitely happened. While Mom was snoring in her sleep, Dad was on the veranda, smoking as he looked out at the garden. Dad's hair was still black and his shoulders were massive, she was sure of that. Wasn't that just a bit before he left their family?

When he looked out into the darkness as he smoked, what had her dad been thinking? Had he been thinking about Tae, this new woman from Izu? About the fate of the wife and the two children he was going to leave behind? Even if she and Kazuo became husband and wife, would there be nights like those?

Suddenly a large shadow appeared standing behind Kazuo. It was Yūzō. He stretched out his hand and abruptly stroked Kazuo's head.

"There's a lump." He rubbed it again. "I've always been strong. When we used to thumb-wrestle in the staff room, there wasn't a single person who could take me on." Yūzō extended his hand as if challenging Kazuo.

Yūzō's watery, bluish eyes gleamed in the darkness, neither laughing nor crying.

Kazuo flung his lit cigarette into the garden and stuck out his own hand.

"So?"

"Yeah, you are strong."

"Aren't I?"

The two of them thumb-wrestled, occasionally grunting and tossing comments and forth. It was a ritual in which they accepted and forgave each other. Motoko poked Kumiko awake. Motoko felt as if someone both she and her sister cared about deeply had been accepted. Strangely, the grudge that Motoko bore against her sister would hide somewhere, seeming to vanish, during times like these.

The snoring they could hear from the next room was Tae's. She was always saying, "I ruined a former principal's life" and "my crimes are serious, aren't they?"

Tae put on those dramatic airs with great emotion. She seemed to fancy herself something of a wicked seductress, but because of her weight and thick neck, she really just looked like a cylindrical wooden *kokeshi* doll.

Motoko didn't know how it came to be like this, but she wondered if these days—being waited on by a young, cheerful woman, living in a place with good air, from time to time taking a peek into their customers' luggage and then getting scolded for it—were perhaps the happiest times of her father's life.

Tae spoke loudly in her sleep.

THE OPENING DAY OF Kumiko's store had been fixed.

It was a Japanese-style snack bar named Kōji, located on a main street. Even for this tiny shop, just about a hundred and eighty square feet, they worked straight through the night before opening day. It would have been a different story if the store had been equipped with all its furnishings, including plates and utensils, but as it was she had to buy small bowls and plates that were at least serviceable, check that nothing was broken once the china store delivered them, take the price tags off the dishes, wash them, and organize them on the shelves. That alone was a huge job.

"I remember the first time. . ." began Kumiko.

"You forgot the abacus, remember?" Motoko,

having come to help, spoke as Kumiko sorted delivery receipts from the liquor store.

"Not just the abacus. Didn't I forget something more important?"

"Oh yeah. . ."

It was exactly ten years ago. Kumiko had opened a shop on a backstreet of Kamata. It was a restaurant serving coffee and curry, in an inexpensive space they had rented next to a floundering tatami mat store. After they opened the shop, ten minutes went by, then twenty, without any customers. People did look into the store, over and over, but nobody pushed open the door and came in. Their father was gone, and Motoko, Kumiko, and their mother had to eat somehow. This was their last stand. Motoko felt her face stiffening.

"I put a lot of thought into creating an atmosphere that would be inviting to customers, but maybe something's stopping them from just opening the door and coming in."

"Let's go outside and look at the place from a customer's perspective."

With those words, Kumiko and Motoko went outside and gasped in surprise. It was obvious why the customers weren't coming in. The sign was swaying in the wind: "Closed (Sorry, We're Still Getting Ready)."

They reminisced over the story, laughing hard; it felt like even in heaven, there wouldn't be anything that could replace their sisterhood.

THE DOOR FLEW OPEN and Mr. Yagisawa came in. He owned the store. He was the one who had poached Kumiko from a bar in Kinshichō, where she had been hired as the lead hostess.

"Is the principal coming for the opening?"

Yagisawa owned two or three shabby arcades and snack bars in the area. He had overextended himself to the point where his creditors were always after him. He was constantly busy, but as a former student of Yūzō's, he continued to call him "Principal" even now.

"Why would he come? I don't think he wants to watch his own daughter pour drinks for men."

"Nah, that's just how he used to be. People change completely with their environments."

"Some change but some don't."

"I guess so. Some people will keep a secret pearl of consistency in their chest, and that aspect of them will remain unchanged."

Yagisawa had long ago shown signs of having fallen in love with Kumiko. Her ten years of experience in the nightlife business were evident in the way she lightly dodged Yagisawa's advances. Apparently they'd been neither together nor apart for quite some time.

Motoko was more concerned about her sister's words. What did she mean when she said that some people don't change?

"Motoko, you've really gotten pretty," said Yagisawa.

"Of course she has. She's *getting ready*," said Kumiko.

Kumiko stopped, smiled at Yagisawa, and looked at the door sign.

"You know him, Mr. Yagisawa." When Motoko said Kazuo's name, Yagisawa made a sound like something was stuck in his throat and looked into Kumiko's eyes.

"*Mama-san*," he said hoarsely and blinked two or

three times. He seemed to be both in disbelief and asking if *mama-san* approved of this situation.

Yagisawa knew something too. Everybody knew, but nobody would say anything. They would rattle on and on about mindless things, but when it came to something crucial they would shut their mouths tight like clams and sink into silence. Even if a woman was writhing in agony because of their silence, they just passed right by as if they hadn't even noticed.

Motoko had intended to help out at her sister's store even if it meant taking some time off from her dressmaking. She couldn't stay with Kazuo all the time; he was working at the factory. But even more than that, it was better to be at her sister's side. If there was something between them and if it still lingered, then surely Motoko would find out about it as long as she stuck to one of them like glue.

Motoko was diligently peeling the price tags off the small bowls and washing them thoroughly.

"Thanks for helping, Motoko. Are you going to help us when we open too?" asked Yagisawa. Motoko was used to the way he put things. "It's a waste for you to stay in Japan. If you went to a foreign country, Motoko, you'd have your pick of guys."

It's just like this, just like with the odors of different cheeses; the people who like them can't get enough, but there are also people who dislike them. Yagisawa's real meaning was: Please don't come to the store to help out on opening day.

"Thanks for asking, but when you open I'll just visit as a customer," she reassured him.

There had been no messages from Kazuo since she'd returned from Izu. Maybe he was hesitating because of her sister's presence. In any case, she'd invite Kazuo to the opening tomorrow and they'd go together. If she could, she'd sit next to Kazuo and have her sister pour them a version of the *sansankudo* nuptial sake.

UNFORTUNATELY, IT RAINED THE next night, the evening of Kōji's opening. It wasn't a nice night to be out and there were hardly any customers. Motoko had dragged Kazuo there. Aside from them and the uncomfortable-looking Yagisawa, who was neither really behind nor in front of the counter, there were only two older men, drinking gloomily as they ran their eyes over a horse-racing paper.

Yagisawa was dressed smartly in a white coat that night. He was a cheap guy, but Motoko always felt strangely suffocated when she was alone with a man like him in an elevator. Saliva would build up in her mouth, and when she tried to swallow without him noticing, she would make a gulping sound.

Maybe she found him attractive.

Kumiko didn't look much at Kazuo. She poured beer for the customers and spoke to Motoko and Yagisawa. Kazuo touched the artificial flowers, chain-smoked, and chimed in when Motoko spoke to him. It was Yagisawa instead who was attentive to Kazuo, lighting his cigarettes for him.

"How about this? Why you don't get Yagisawa over here for a drink?" After she said it, the rest came easily. "Kumiko, would you pour for us?"

"You don't have to ask. It's my job."

"This isn't really business, though. It's special."

"Special?"

"I'd hate to make any kind of big ceremony, so. . ."

"You mean *sansankudo*?"

"I was thinking that would be great if you could

do it." Then she said to Kazuo, "But I bet it would be tough for you to deal with our father, right?"

Motoko wanted to make Kazuo say something in front of her sister. "No, not at all," or some evasive words. Anything would be fine.

"I like your father," was all Kazuo said.

Kumiko silently poured sake for Kazuo, then for Motoko.

Yagisawa said nothing and lit a new cigarette.

Just then a customer flung open the door and came right in. It was a young man who looked like a laborer. He was drunk, breathing heavily as he leaned on the doorframe.

"Welcome to Kōji," Kumiko called out as she chipped ice, but then she said "Oh!" with surprise. "You came all the way from Kinshichō?"

He must have walked over without an umbrella, because his head and shoulders were wet. Kumiko came out from behind the counter with a hand towel.

"Anyway, it must have been hard to find us." As she said it, she made to wipe the man's shoulders with the towel. The man made a deep, throaty noise and leaned on Kumiko. Suddenly he winced and Kumiko stumbled.

Motoko thought that maybe Kumiko had stepped on the man's foot. The man took two or three steps back, then threw himself against the door and ran outside. He was holding something shiny, but in that instant Motoko didn't realize what it was. Thinking that something wasn't quite right, Motoko started to stand up, but Kumiko let out a laugh—or rather, she mumbled laughingly, "Looks like I've been stabbed."

Blood was dripping from her left upper arm, leaving red spots on her white summer kimono.

Motoko felt like she was watching a movie in slow motion. It seemed like the whole thing happened in the blink of an eye.

Then there were screaming voices and confused scrambling.

Yagisawa shouted for an ambulance and for someone to call 911. Motoko cried, "A cloth! A cloth! If we don't hurry she's going to bleed out!" and pressed a dishcloth against the wound.

The customers left the store and chased after the man.

Kazuo was the only one who acted differently. He froze completely, as if his hands and feet were tied in place, and turned pale, standing and staring at Kumiko. If some third party had walked in just then, he would surely have thought that Kazuo was the one who'd been stabbed.

Kumiko turned to Kazuo and muttered, "I don't even know that man's name. I don't know why he'd do something like that."

The man turned himself in at the local police station right away. They said that he entered silently, softly put the knife on the desk of the young policeman who was writing in the police log, and said, "Please give me some water."

IT WOULD BE TEN days before Kumiko's wound was completely healed. A large blood vessel had been damaged, and her profuse bleeding had frightened her senseless, but she'd be able to go back to work in the store in a week.

Yagisawa was worked up when he came back from the police station. "It's a horrible story. The man's name is Kikumoto. Seems like he used to frequent the bar in Kinshichō. He became obsessed with *mama-san* and sat down at the counter and asked her to marry him. She's a hostess and entertaining people is her job, so she couldn't directly refuse him. So she said, 'Ok, that's great, I'm so happy you asked.' She just let him hold her hand. They had this exchange every night. I guess he took it seriously. He said that when she moved here suddenly, she just trampled all over his feelings. But it doesn't seem like he wanted to kill her. It's a good thing she wasn't more seriously injured."

Motoko and Yagisawa had met at the hospital entrance and were taking the elevator up to Kumiko's room together.

"In the end, we're sisters. Once I realized that she wasn't in danger, I cried so much."

The two of them stepped out of the elevator and entered the nurses' station to ask for Kumiko's room number.

"It was really strange. Those tears felt like hot water."

"It's because the two of you have the same blood in your veins."

The nurses' station was empty. Maybe the nurses were making their night rounds, checking the patients' temperatures.

As Motoko and Yagisawa were leaving the nurses' station, they suddenly heard Kumiko's voice.

"I deserved to be stabbed." Kumiko's muffled voice echoed through the deserted nurses' station. "There really is a God. I received divine punishment." The voice was being transmitted from her room over the intercom. "It was punishment for what happened that time ten years ago."

Yagisawa, who had entered after Motoko, stared slack-jawed at Motoko's face.

"No, it's not. It's absolutely not. If God punished anyone, he would punish my brother. And me." It was Kazuo. His voice had an intensity that Motoko had never heard before.

Yagisawa reached to press the red "off" button on the intercom. But Motoko took his hand and pressed it to her breast, holding it there.

"It's my brother's fault for dumping you like that at the last moment."

"But that doesn't mean I had to make that mistake with his younger brother."

"It wasn't a mistake."

"It was. Even if it only happened once, that's what society calls a mistake."

"You're wrong. It's a wonderful thing."

Motoko felt her body begin to tremble.

"I'm the one who started it."

"No, it was me."

Motoko would be mortified if Yagisawa perceived her trembling, but she had to listen until the end.

"It's something I'll never forget," said Kazuo.

"You have to forget it. If you don't, it'll be so terrible for Motoko."

"I feel bad about it. But it's like the memory's been seared into me with red-hot tongs. The scar from that burn lingers so clearly and won't go away."

"It's the same with me. The pain from that is worse than my stab wound."

"We shouldn't be talking about this."

"It's fine. This is the last time we'll ever talk alone. Otherwise, I'll feel so bad for Motoko."

And then the voices that had come through the intercom were silent. Motoko's breathing became labored. She didn't care how painful the conversation might be; she wanted them to say something.

There was something terrifying and excruciating about silence.

"You really like Motoko, don't you?"

"I do." It wasn't the intense voice from before. It was Kazuo's usual tone.

"The other day, we were together at the Hachiman shrine. When I saw her shoulders as she prayed next to me, I suddenly started to cry. What is she praying for? She's totally devoted, but no good has ever come of it. If things stay like this for her, it's just too sad."

It seemed like Kazuo was going to say something, but then the intercom was cut off. An elderly nurse who had come in flicked it off with a businesslike gesture and looked dubiously at the two of them standing there.

Motoko walked down the long hallway toward Kumiko's room. She marveled that her feet were moving her forward by themselves. Even though she had rejected the wild ideas in her head, the idea that she couldn't fully deny had turned out to be true. Ten years ago, Kazuo had shared a period of bliss with her sister.

"You're surprised, aren't you?" It was Yagisawa.

Motoko said she wasn't surprised. "I had a feeling about it."

"Then why'd this happen? If you knew that he'd done that with your sister, even just once—you should have stayed away from him."

Motoko gave a small laugh and asked if Yagisawa had ever skied. When you cross a steep slope, if you put your weight on your downhill foot, you'll fall down the mountain. It's the same principle.

"It's dangerous over there. And the more I think about that, the more I end up going there. When I think of how I should avoid him of all people, I'm attracted to him all the more."

Yagisawa nodded.

"That does happen. But—" He stopped walking. "You can't catch happiness that way."

Instead of answering him, Motoko smiled. Instead of crying, she smiled with all her might.

"I probably shouldn't say this, but I've thought for a really long time that your sister was the pretty one. But you're also pretty. You have a nice face."

Today was the first time Motoko had heard either Kazuo's or Yagisawa's tone become so serious. Motoko and Yagisawa paused in front of the door to Kumiko's room. They waited for a moment and then opened the door.

Kumiko was half sitting up on the bed with her left hand in a sling, and Kazuo was sitting in a chair at the window, a little way off from the bed. They both looked calm.

Motoko cried in a bright, carefree voice, "Oh, Kazuo! Here you are."

Yagisawa, not to be outdone, enthusiastically relayed new information: "They caught the guy who did it."

As Motoko placed the toiletries she had brought at her sister's bedside, she suddenly smelled that odor. The odor that would make her cringe every summer. For a moment, Motoko thought it was her own smell, but then she realized it wasn't.

It was Kumiko.

Half in doubt, Motoko whispered, "Kumiko, want me to bring you a damp washcloth?"

"Do I smell?" Her older sister laughed lightly. "I smell when I get nervous. Apparently our grandmother was the same way. I think they call that atavism."

WHEN THEY LEFT THE hospital, the odors of the neighborhood suddenly advanced on them from the darkness. The lights were off in both the big and small factories. The daytime glow from the lathes and milling machines had vanished as well, and the machines were sleeping quietly. But even though the machines were dormant, the daytime odors persisted. Maybe machines breathed in their sleep like people, or maybe the lingering scent from the daytime had intensified once again in the darkness.

Motoko, Kazuo, and Yagisawa all walked silently. Yagisawa stopped in front of a vending machine and bought three cans of beer.

They continued to walk as they drank the beers.

"It makes me really frustrated to watch you," Yagisawa said to Kazuo without looking at him. "If you're in love, then be in love. Why don't you just say it outright?"

In a muffled voice, Kazuo said only, "I can't say what I don't know."

A cat crossed in front of the three of them. Where was it going, and to do what? Was it male or female? Judging by how it moved, it was probably still young. It disappeared inside a dilapidated factory dorm.

"You can't see feelings," said Kazuo.

"You can't see them, so you can't understand them?"

Kazuo silently slurped the froth from his beer.

"But I guess the people who do it, they just do it. Even if they don't understand, even if they can't see—because they don't understand, because they can't see, they do it all the more. You can't compare to that man, the man who stabbed *mama-san* tonight."

In a conversation without any replies, the footsteps of the three of them became the questions and answers.

"What he did was absurd. But at least he's more of a man than you."

Yagisawa seemed to be getting more and more irritated at Kazuo's silence.

"I don't have a right to criticize him either. He's much better than me." Then Yagisawa shouted as if he were slapping Kazuo. "You're garbage!"

In a louder voice, he shouted again: "I'm scum too!"

He threw his beer can toward the dilapidated factory dorm in a grand motion and then casually lifted his hand. In a softer voice, he said, "Give my regards to the principal. That man is the best."

With that, he walked away. Motoko was a little bit amused.

Kumiko had asked that they not tell her father about the incident, and so they hadn't contacted anybody in Izu. Right about then, their elderly father was surely sleeping in his run-down house by the seashore with his fat lover who was young enough to be his daughter. He would rise from bed softly in the middle of the night, quietly open one of the travel bags they had been entrusted with, pull out its contents, and look at them.

He was scolded by his young lover, humiliated by her. That was the nature of old age. A return to spring.

Motoko searched for Kazuo's hand. His fingers were stout. They were reticent fingers, hiding his thoughts. But they were unmistakably a man's fingers. While she was searching for his fingers, she felt as if fingers were a man's body. Kazuo gripped her hand tightly in return. Finally, Motoko realized what had transpired.

That time, the first time, when Kazuo had said that he smelled like oil and Motoko had returned the favor by embracing his head and pushing her armpit up against him. Maybe Kazuo was thinking about Kumiko. His face was peaceful because he was remembering that one-time bliss that he had shared ten years earlier with Motoko's sister.

The wind had stopped and the smell from the canals had intensified.

"It's high tide." Kazuo never spoke about the essential things. Maybe he liked to put the important things inside his heart and body and let life take its course.

"You can't catch happiness that way." She could hear Yagisawa's voice. Rather than stagnating in anguish next to a man in whom the heart and body of her sister still lived, maybe going to the sea—it wasn't exactly the flow of a river, but still—and crossing it to live in another world would be more like the happiness that people spoke of.

But Motoko believed in the power of Kazuo's fingers as they returned her grip, and she wanted to stay here a little longer. Every day was painful, but it was the painful times, the days when she cried and cursed, when she felt more alive. Wasn't this happiness as well?

If Kazuo didn't let go of her hand, Motoko would go back to his house with him. She wouldn't mind if her sister showed up with a disgusted expression. She wanted to enter Kazuo's house in silence. She wanted to sleep next to him until morning.

The Walnut Room

THE WEDDING ENDED WITHOUT incident.

It went well, if I do say so myself, Momoko wanted to gush, but she wasn't the one getting married. It was her colleague Rie. A year younger than Momoko, she was a twenty-nine-year-old bride. Momoko's role was that of the bride's close friend. Though she wasn't particularly proud of it, this was a role she was accustomed to, and she hadn't thought this would be anything new. And yet today had been a little hard on her. Perhaps because it could have been Momoko herself sitting in the bride's chair.

"The bridegroom, Mr. Sekiguchi, is the number two in my editing department. But among us ladies he's number one. Because he's a second son who graduated from a second-rate university, he isn't intimidating, and that's just perfect. The fact that he isn't handsome makes us feel self-confident. The new girls in the office can use their youth. Women with prosperous parents, property, and houses use their financial assets. And leftover inventory like me just has the truth to work with. Of course it's just my own assessment, but I think I was on the right track. Yes, that's right. One night when he was drunk and on his way home from working over-time, Mr. Sekiguchi grabbed my hand tightly in front of a love hotel. If I hadn't poked fun at him and said 'Wow, what a grip!' I'd be wearing the white veil in the bride's seat today. . . ."

Momoko had gone red just at the thought of what the reaction would be at the reception if she were to give that speech. But of course the whole thing had been only a murmur in her head before she practiced her speech the previous night.

The real Momoko had rehearsed with a three-minute sand timer she'd won in a raffle at the supermarket at the end of last year. She gave the best speech she could, appearing joyful and giving the impression that she was the person who most deeply understood the bride and groom. She received the appropriate applause and, speaking in such a happy way, she became actually happy, her voice shaking with emotion at the ends of her sentences. Perhaps that was one of Momoko's quirks.

The bride looked as though she'd been crying. Many of the guests apparently thought she'd been crying during the ceremonial exchange of nuptial cups because she had achieved her goal of marriage just a hair's breadth from her thirtieth birthday, but that wasn't it. The reality was that there had been a disturbance in the makeup room.

As part of the traditional change of dress during the reception, Rie had been changing into a borrowed bridal kimono. She was having the hairdressing and her hairpiece done in the hotel's makeup room but had decided to do the makeup herself without any help from a professional. Momoko had recommended that, but Rie had looked dissatisfied.

"The makeup fee is only a thousand yen. This happens once in a lifetime, so I want to have it done for me."

"Since it's once in a lifetime, you'd better do

it yourself. It won't be your own face if you have someone else do it for you."

"You'd better do this. You'd better do that," were Momoko's favorite phrases.

"You think so, huh."

"You know your own face better than anybody. It's the face you've had for thirty years, and there's no reason to entrust it to someone else on the most important day of your life."

"Hey, I'm twenty-nine."

"Anyway, are you really okay being one of those package brides they show all together in those commercials for wedding halls? If I were in your shoes I'd definitely hate that."

When Momoko got involved in another person's business, she really felt like she was stepping into that person's shoes. She would steamroll through any opposition.

Since early morning, Momoko had been in constant, devoted attendance on Rie, who had no female relatives. In the makeup room, Rie wrapped a white cloth around her neck and was patting it down when she exclaimed "Oh!" and spun her hand around as if she were doing the *awa-odori* dance performed at festivals.

"This is awful. I forgot it!" She was missing her eyelash curler.

With a light laugh, Momoko took one out of her bag and placed it on the vanity.

"I thought this might happen and brought one with me. Good thing it came in handy."

Rie gazed at Momoko with a face like that of a pure white sheep.

"You've really done everything for me."

"Don't worry about it. Hurry up."

With her mouth half open, Rie put her face right up against the mirror and was curling her eyelashes, but then she let out another cry. This exclamation was more serious than the previous one.

One of Rie's eyelashes was entirely gone. It had stuck to and been torn off by the eyelash curler Momoko had lent her. The rubber on the part of the curler that rolled up the eyelashes had oxidized and become soft and sticky, probably from age. Rie had carefully and tightly wrapped her eyelash around it, and apparently the lash had gotten stuck.

"What should I do? I can't go out with my face like this!"

Rie was sobbing on the vanity table, and Momoko gave her a hearty slap on the back.

"I'm not going to apologize. In the time I would use to apologize, I'll go to the arcade downstairs, get some false eyelashes, and bring them right back."

As she was rushing out of the makeup room, Momoko thought, *If I were a guy, I guess this is one of those times when I'd say "Serves you right." I see the gods really are here. They're delivering divine punishment to the person who's stolen from somebody else.* But that sentiment only lasted for a moment, and then she ran as fast as she could.

Momoko realized for the first time that there are fake eyelashes for the right and left eyes. Both Momoko and Rie usually put on quick and simple makeup, so they didn't really know how to stick the lashes on. In the end, they got help from the professional in the makeup room.

"You know, we have some eyelashes here. If you'd just told me before," the makeup artist had said. In the end, Momoko had to tip her a thousand yen, tucking the bill into a gift envelope.

This always happened to Momoko. She would involve herself for someone else's sake when she wasn't needed. She would do everything she could, go too far, and then it would backfire. So when things went wrong, that would also be her responsibility. She was always losing out. This time, too, it was Momoko who paid the eighteen hundred yen for the false eyelashes.

"Hmm, I wonder if they'll be all right at night."

"Huh?"

"The eyelashes, I wonder if they'll stay on."

"It's a special glue, so I think they should be fine. And if not, you'll already be husband and wife, so fessing up could be good for your future relationship."

Momoko even consulted with Rie in total seriousness about what would happen that night, though she should have told Rie to figure that much out for herself. It was a ridiculous conversation, when Momoko thought about it, but anyhow, Rie didn't notice the feelings that Momoko was hiding. Momoko was able to see the newlyweds off with a wish for their happiness as they departed for their honeymoon from Tokyo Station.

After that, it looked like her colleagues from the editorial department were setting out for a karaoke bar.

"Sorry, but there's somewhere I have to be." Momoko had a knack for purposely dropping her voice and speaking casually.

"Are you going to Uguisudani again?"

"Do wedding ceremonies make you want to go visit your boyfriend?"

These days, Momoko had acquired a way of meaningfully laughing with just her eyes without saying yes or no and then walking away. And that's how she found herself sitting on the platform at Uguisudani Station.

When things became unbearable, when the strained threads felt like they were about to snap, Momoko would go to sit on a bench at Uguisudani Station.

There was no boyfriend. There was, however, her father, who lived a ten-minute walk away, with a young woman.

Momoko's father had left the house three years ago. He had been a strait-laced man working at a midlevel pharmaceutical company and living with Momoko and her mother, little brother, and little sister. They were a five-person family that didn't know the meaning of luxury but also wasn't struggling to make ends meet.

Then one day her father went to work and simply didn't come back. He wasn't the kind of person who would play mah-jongg all night or sleep away from home. Momoko's mother worried that there had been an accident and called the office the next day, only to find out that the company had gone bankrupt a month earlier.

"Dad could never show his weakness. Even when he was hung over, he would cover his mouth with his hand and head to work. He probably had trouble telling us that his company had failed."

"It's your fault, Mom. You're constantly telling me to look at Dad's example and putting him on a pedestal. He had nowhere to hide."

This mother-daughter quarrel was past its usefulness.

For three months, they heard not a single word from her father. Her mother lost a little bit of weight every day. Momoko, at a complete loss, went to visit Tsuzuki, who had been a subordinate of her father's.

"This could be suicide, and I'm thinking it might be better to request a police search."

They were meeting in an unfashionable coffee shop. There was a film clinging to the surface of Momoko's lukewarm coffee. Tsuzuki was a decade younger than her father, so he would be forty soon. As he chain-smoked, he said, "Mr. Mitamura is alive." He mumbled it, as if it were hard to say.

Tsuzuki said that her father was living in a squalid apartment at the end of an alley in Uguisudani. At that point, as if to cut Momoko off before she started to shriek, *What's he doing there*, Tsuzuki blew a smoke ring and mumbled something else.

"He's not alone."

There was a Renoir hanging on the wall behind Tsuzuki. It was a cheap reproduction. A round, fat young woman was exposing her breasts, but she was looking at the viewer with a vacant expression. The frame was a little warped.

"She's thirty-five or thirty-six. She runs an *oden* shop—supposedly it's just one step above a street stall—the *mama-san* of this shop is the woman I hear he's living with.

If Momoko remembered correctly, Renoir took a maid as his wife. Maybe this model was that maid. An image of the artist, past middle age and with thinning hair, sneaking into the maid's quarters by night flickered before Momoko's eyes. The face of the elderly artist had become just like her father's.

Momoko asked Tsuzuki to take her to the apartment.

"I think you're better off not going. To a man, this is a matter of honor, and Mr. Mitamura has a doubly strong sense of that. I don't think you should make a big deal of this. Just wait for a better time."

Momoko refused to back down. She only wanted to know the location of the apartment just in case. She definitely wouldn't go inside. "My father has high blood pressure, and just in case the unthinkable happens, I'd like to see him before he dies."

Tsuzuki reached for the check with a resigned expression.

THE SUN WAS ALREADY setting by the time Momoko stood in front of the ancient mortar-and-wood apartment building. There was a large shoe rack in the common area out front, like what one might find in an elementary school, and there were children's sneakers and sandals scattered about the dirt floor.

Tsuzuki patted Momoko on the back as if to say, "All right, time to go," but Momoko shook off his hand. She started to walk toward the vacant strip of land, wide enough for just one person to pass through, bordering one side of the building. The first window she saw was open.

A man's hand reached out and pulled inside the woman's underpants and brassiere that had been drying on the windowsill.

"Dad." Even Momoko didn't understand why she'd said it; the wooden plank placed across the window prevented her from seeing the man's face.

He pulled the underwear into the house and the glass window made a noise when it shut.

Momoko began to scream, "Anybody home? Anybody there?" while banging on the wooden plank.

"Enough for today. Let's go," said Tsuzuki, trying to tear her away.

Momoko leapt at Tsuzuki's chest, rubbing her forehead against it and calming her ragged breathing. When she looked back over her shoulder as they left, she saw that faded curtains had been drawn behind the glass window.

When there was an emergency, Momoko tended to be more zealous than necessary. She'd noticed this trait before, but from that night forward it was much more intense. She felt like she was poised for battle.

MOMOKO GOT OFF THE train at Meguro station and called her house from a pay phone. It was her little sister Yōko, a ninth grader, who answered.

"Did you have dinner?"

"We were waiting for you but we got hungry, so just a moment ago we were saying we should start eating."

"Good. I have really happy news, so I'm going to treat you to eel. Wait for me."

"What's the happy news?"

"I'll tell you while we eat."

Their meals had become quite meager since their father had stopped showing up for dinner. It had been a long time since they'd eaten something like *unajū*, broiled eel over rice.

"Did you get a raise?" asked Momoko's mother. Her mother said that she didn't need the eel and that it was a waste to buy it for her, but nonetheless she chewed at it slowly. Momoko's brother, Kentarō, who was going through a third round of applications for college, was wolfing it down so fast that it caught in his throat.

Her sister joked, "For some reason I'm getting a bad feeling about this. Don't tell me we're going to have to commit a midnight family suicide."

Momoko broke in with deliberate cheerfulness. "Dad's alive and well."

Everybody's chopsticks froze.

"I think that he might be planning on coming home if he finds work."

Her mother put down the *unajū*.

"Where is he?"

"Somewhere downtown."

"Where downtown?"

"Apparently he's not living alone." Chewing exaggeratedly, Momoko produced a light laugh. "I heard he's living with a woman. Up until now he was totally devoted, walking straight down this one road, right? But when his company failed, that took him by surprise and suddenly he turned onto a side street. When they suffer a setback like that, it's actually unfaithful people who have a better ability to fight back. But Dad didn't have any antibodies."

Momoko broke off, and in the silence she became worried about her mother. Momoko's mother had reached the cusp of old age in total earnestness and without any particular hobbies of her own while managing the family finances, serving her husband devotedly, and raising her children. Even without her husband missing, she was cranky and moody.

While Momoko said jokingly, "Well, this woman seems to be the *mama-san* of a small *oden* shop, and Dad likes *oden*, so maybe that's why he fooled around," she peered at her mother's *unajū*.

Eel was her mother's favorite dish. If she ate it all, things would be all right going forward. Somehow she would be able to struggle through this.

"Mom, you're probably angry, but for Dad I think this is like a vacation. If we try to barge into his house, it'll be our loss. Let's all cheer up and just wait for him." Thinking about it afterwards, Momoko could only call her remarks impertinent, though she had said them in earnest at the time.

"Is *bancha* all right?" Her mother was asking about a variety of coarse green tea. That was all she said. It was her usual voice. Her *unajū* was all gone.

"Huh? I thought *bancha* didn't go well with eel."

"You're such a fool. It's pickled plum that you're not supposed to pair with eel." Her mother laughed and suddenly got up and dashed into the kitchen.

At the sound of her mother vomiting, Momoko got up and went to her. She was gasping as she gripped the sink. She had thrown up all of her food.

"You didn't have to say all that in front of Kentarō and Yōko!" She glared at Momoko, a strand of saliva hanging from her mouth. Momoko noticed for the first time that her mother had *uesanpaku* eyes; the whites of her mother's eyes were visible not just to the sides of the irises but also above them.

"Sorry. I thought they'd figure it out sooner or later."

I understood that it was something to tell you alone, but if I did that the conversation would surely get dark and serious. I was afraid you might become hysterical and say "You know where he is, don't you? Take me there this instant!" I thought that would be even worse. So from now on, I'll deliver bad news in a deliberately loud voice as if it's amusing. If I don't do that, I don't think we can make it through this— Momoko rubbed her mother's back as if to express all those feelings.

Her mother shook off Momoko's hand and grumbled, "I did all I could for him, you know. What was he unhappy about?"

Momoko wanted to tell her mother that her total devotion was the problem.

"SOMEBODY IN THIS HOUSE just doesn't get humor."

Her father had said that at some point while sitting at the dinner table. Her father was a person completely lacking any affinity for, interest in, or appreciation of humor, so Momoko thought his comment was funny. Her mother, however, coming in from the kitchen carrying a bottle of soy sauce, couldn't disregard her husband's remarks and took the comment seriously.

"Were you talking about me just then?"

"I never said it was you."

"So who were you talking about?"

"Let's forget it."

"No, we won't. Please explain it to me clearly."

"You just won't let matters be. That's what it means to have no sense of humor."

If Momoko had been a step removed, this too might have been humorous. But instead she felt like it might be this kind of interaction that made her disappointed father loath to return home.

Momoko's mother was an attentive woman. She liked keeping things neat and tidy, and she would say that she would never be embarrassed if someone opened any of her drawers. She took care of the household finances without misplacing a single yen, and she disliked ambiguities, even in everyday matters. If something wasn't set out clearly in black and white, she wasn't satisfied. Even when she was dressing up in a kimono, she couldn't wear the collar loosely. She would secure it tightly around her neck.

Of course, the *mama-san* of the *oden* shop who was living with Momoko's father couldn't be exactly the same as the woman Momoko had seen in the Renoir in the coffee shop, but she probably fastened her collar sloppily and had a loose character.

Momoko's brother and sister waited in the living room with anxious expressions. Her mother retched again, making a miserable noise. Rubbing her mother's bony back, Momoko relinquished a lot of her inner hopes. Love that would ripen in a moment if she only did the right thing. Dressing in a smart, feminine style. She resolved to draw a red line from that day forward like she was closing an account book at the end of the year.

Her brother would have to go to college. She had seen the handicap their father had suffered as a night school graduate, so Kentarō would get into a full college program come hell or high water. And she wanted Yōko to make it through high school without having to worry about money.

It's all right, your sister is here. Momoko jokingly beat her chest like an alpha-male gorilla.

Happiness won't come walking this way
So I'll go walking to it

The words were those of Kiyoko Suizenji, a singer and actress. Until then, Momoko wouldn't have given Kiyoko the time of day. Momoko had scorned her coarse clothing and unrefined way of singing.

But soon they'd have to leave their company housing. When they applied for public housing, when they looked for a cheap apartment, when they had to go get an official registration of the family seal—at times like those, Debussy or the stylish musician Yōsui Inoue would be hopelessly lacking in authority. For the times when Momoko changed into her flats, puffed out her chest, and walked forward with courage, Kiyoko Suizenji was the best.

One step in one day, three steps in three days
Forward three steps and back two

That was how the next three years passed. Irresistible force and foolhardiness. Momoko was a lion one day and a wild boar the next. Even at her office, she said nothing of her father having left home.

She became an even merrier drinker than before. Her colleagues gossiped about this Momoko who laughed often and worked briskly: "Has something good happened to her?"

When they took overnight company trips to ski or to swim in the ocean, Momoko was the only one who didn't go.

"I'm kind of busy. . . ." She would giggle suggestively and give her coworkers some chocolates or other treats to take with them, but she wouldn't join the group. The rumors bounced around: "Seems like Ms. Mitamura's got a special someone." A woman with a lover would tell her parents that she was going on a business trip and then the two of them would go alone somewhere else to ski or enjoy the ocean. At this, Momoko felt a bit of vanity and pride.

When she was wearing her old, pilling sweater, she was less miserable if she smiled with seeming mirth. When she found something even a little funny, she would think, *I'll laugh while I have the chance.* She wanted to cheer herself up with laughter.

When she laughed meaningfully and skipped the trips, it was because she couldn't bear the expense. When she had spare time, she was better off helping her mother with some hemming, part of her mother's part-time dressmaking work. She was completely blocked at every turn.

No matter how long she waited, her father never came home. When Momoko would come back from work and see the windows of her apartment building, it seemed that the lights in their apartment were dimmer than all the others.

She would take a deep breath in front of the door and say, "I'm home!" Then she would enter the apartment with lots of energy.

For her mother, who liked sweet things, she would often bring home a parcel of broiled sweet chestnuts or a cheap cake. She couldn't bring home good news, so she wanted to bring home something warm or sweet instead.

Only when her mother was chewing would the complaints cease. It probably wasn't entirely due to Momoko's use of food to stop the grievances, but her mother began eating often.

When it came to food, her mother had been on the abstemious side. But now she would say, "I just can't stand it," as she opened the fridge. "I don't care if your father doesn't come back."

She started having a small bottle of beer at night.

After a year passed this way, she said to Momoko, "Aren't the sashes for kimono getting short these days?" But the sashes hadn't gotten any shorter. Momoko's mother had gained weight.

Her little brother Kentarō blocked out the sounds of their mother's sewing machine with earplugs while studying assiduously for his entrance examinations. He was admitted to a college engineering department, second-tier though it was.

Kentarō knew about absolutely nothing other than chemistry and physics. Once, when he was eating roasted smelt, called *wakasagi*, he remarked in surprise, "Wait, so this is *wakasagi*? Since *wakai* means 'young' and *sagi* means 'heron,' I always thought *wakasagi* was the meat of a young heron."

"You've had *wakasagi* before."

"I always thought that was just full-grown whitebait."

It was a waste to ask a boy like him about the subtleties of romance.

He wasn't the type to do the right thing and devote himself to a part-time job while juggling his college lectures to help out his older sister, but on the other hand, he also didn't get sucked into the radical student movement or get involved with women.

Nor was Momoko's little sister, Yōko, a source of support. She was, after all, only a high school student, so there wasn't much to do about it, but Yōko was worse than just unreliable; Momoko couldn't let the girl out of her sight.

It wasn't fair to say that she was a washout or a failure, but there was something lax about her character. When she wanted something, she was indiscriminate. As a child she would often take two or three ice cream boxes from the front of the candy store and bring them home. Their mother would bring money to the store and apologize. There was also an incident where she followed a goldfish vendor somewhere, and the police got involved in that. Her grades were also outstandingly awful.

"If we can find a willing candidate, anyone would be fine. We've got to turn her into a bride before she does something terrible." Both her mother and father used to say that.

To be a role model for her sister, Momoko had to

conduct herself irreproachably. The only breaths of fresh air available to Momoko were her meetings with Tsuzuki to hear about her father.

"I WONDER WHAT UGUISUDANI's plans are?" For the first year after he left, she'd called him "Dad." The next year, it was "that man." In the third year, Momoko began calling him "Uguisudani."

"Uguisudani." Tsuzuki had also stopped calling him Mr. Mitamura. Tsuzuki himself had been unemployed for about half a year, but he had found work at a foreign pharmaceutical company, and his life seemed to have stabilized. When Momoko broached the subject of her father, Tsuzuki always took out a cigarette and began to smoke.

"Momotarō is with them, so I think that everything's probably fine," said Tsuzuki. Momoko's father had often called her Momotarō, the name of the peach boy hero of Japanese folklore. There might have been in the nickname a hint of his wishing that Momoko had been born a boy.

"That incredibly precocious Momotarō. . ." said Momoko.

"You really are like Momotarō. He took along a dog, a monkey, and a pheasant, and he just wouldn't give up."

"With that white headband."

"You've really done well. I'm impressed."

She felt a warmth inside her chest when Tsuzuki praised her, as if she had just swallowed hot water.

"I bet there are times when you want to throw everything aside and just remove yourself from the situation, right?"

Momoko had heard that there was a hot-water-dispenser called "Just Push," and with Tsuzuki it was exactly like that. Just a trivial word of appreciation for her efforts would make something hot rise up inside her.

At the end of the month, there would always be a phone call for her at the editorial department from Tsuzuki.

"Are you free tonight? If that works for you, let's meet and talk about the usual stuff." The words that came out of the receiver were always the same.

The "usual stuff" was Momoko's father, but advice from Tsuzuki on that topic was only really necessary for the first year.

After consulting Tsuzuki, Momoko had decided that it would be better for her to pretend not to know the location of her father's apartment. But Momoko's mother had ultimately barged into Tsuzuki's new office and insisted on being told where the apartment was. The first year had played host to some fairly dramatic scenes like that.

Momoko had wanted to talk to her father alone, without her mother, and had asked Tsuzuki to be an intermediary. But neither the mother's nor the daughter's efforts proved successful.

"I'm too embarrassed to face her."

"I'm really sorry, but please just pretend that I'm already dead."

These two answers came to her one after the other through Tsuzuki.

If he feared his family marching into his apartment, he should have moved to a new place. But her father didn't move out of his apartment in Uguisudani. Apparently, the *oden* shop run by the woman he was living with was right in the neighborhood.

After their father had been out of the house for six months or so, Momoko became determined to have a face-to-face talk with him. She went to Uguisudani in secret, hiding it even from Tsuzuki. In the late afternoon, about to turn off a main street in front of the train station, she bumped into her father. He had come out of a small supermarket, carrying a shopping basket. Momoko stood stone-still, and her father, wearing a zip-up jacket, was also petrified. Leeks and toilet paper jutted out from his old, amber-colored rattan shopping basket.

This was the same father who, while in their house, had never even bought one pair of his own underwear. Momoko leapt at him and tried to snatch the shopping basket out of his hands.

"I'll carry this for you."

Her father wouldn't hand it over. His eyes looked just about ready to cry, but his expression was otherwise angry. Embracing the basket with remarkable strength, he shook Momoko off. He ignored the traffic light that was about to turn red and ran across the crosswalk to the other side of the street. He lost one of his sandals in the middle of the road but didn't turn back to pick it up. It was a Japanese-style "Hepburn" sandal, a woman's crimson-colored slip-on shoe. Momoko watched it get sucked under the belly of the second or third car to pass by, and with that she walked away.

Momoko phoned Tsuzuki's office from Uguisudani Station. It was the only time Momoko would ever initiate one of their phone calls.

That night, she drank with Tsuzuki for the first time. Until then, they had always had coffee at a café, but from that evening on, it became Tsuzuki's custom to treat her to food and drinks. Drinking wasn't the only first that night; it was also the first time Momoko cried in front of Tsuzuki.

"I wonder if Dad's out of a job."

"He was working at a company that sells fire extinguishers, but apparently there was something fishy about that operation."

So the woman must be supporting him.

Momoko thought her father would probably never come home. After being seen in that state by his daughter, he probably wouldn't come back unless he was dying.

"Do you think what I did was a mistake?"

"No way. You're always in the right, Momoko."

"But it backfired. Whatever I do always backfires."

Tsuzuki laughed, and Momoko was drawn in and laughed too. As she was laughing, she thought of her mother, hunched over, her foot pressing the pedal of her sewing machine. Large tears began to fall from Momoko's eyes like rain on a sunny day.

With her vulnerability exposed, the path was forged. Momoko was no longer particularly embarrassed when she cried in front of Tsuzuki. They would meet once a month, and Momoko came to look forward to getting a little tearful.

When she sat in front of Tsuzuki, Momoko could feel her emotions soften. She would fling off her stiff armor. She would take a break both from being the brave commanding officer, resolved to protect her fortress despite impending defeat, and from being the demon-slaying Momotarō who brought along the useless dog, monkey, and pheasant. She could go back to being the timid girl who had wound up unmarried.

"Order whatever you like." Knowing that Momoko used most of her salary on household expenses, Tsuzuki would always treat her to some good food.

"Seems like he's healthy. Since we've come this far, let's just watch from the sidelines."

Momoko nodded. With that, their "advice" session was over.

"What happened with what you were talking about last time? You said a guy who does translation or something asked you out."

"Oh, don't worry about it. There's this girl who's a much better match for him than I am, so I introduced them. I had two tickets to a game, so I gave them the tickets."

"What? Are you still matchmaking?"

"I'm much more comfortable doing this, and it seems like I've got a talent for it. When I set my sights on a match, it seems it mostly works out in the end even if things get a bit complicated in the middle."

Tsuzuki said nothing and poured beer into Momoko's glass.

Tsuzuki knows everything. I'm better off not letting anything get started rather than being miserable with all of this baggage once things have really gotten serious. In telling herself this and behaving accordingly, it had become second nature for Momoko to avoid getting involved with Tsuzuki.

"Momoko, your problem is that you're just halfway there."

"What do you mean?"

"If you were a peerless beauty, men would come chasing after you—wouldn't matter how far you run, wouldn't even matter if your dad were a murderer."

"I guess so."

"And if you were some hopelessly ugly woman, you'd be very humble so you'd be willing to make a compromise and settle for someone. But you've got average looks, and that's the hardest situation to manage."

He was right on the mark, so Momoko opened her wide mouth and laughed.

Tsuzuki was also average looking. Whether it was his appearance or talent or finances, he was the middle of the middle.

"Tsuzuki, do you have a nickname?"

"No, I guess not. Not even when I was a kid."

"That's no fun."

"People with nicknames are the minority. Get on a train at rush hour and look around. You'll see all these businessmen, the type of people who don't have nicknames, hanging onto the straps and swaying back and forth."

"Now that you mention it, my—" she started to say "father," but corrected herself. "I guess my family members don't have nicknames either."

As she poured beer for Tsuzuki, Momoko asked lightly, "Does your wife have a nickname?"

"Nope, I guess not."

A typical wife with no nickname, and two typical children with no nicknames. A typical tract house. She had connected the bits of what Tsuzuki had told her over these three years, and she could guess at the gist of it.

"The only one with a nickname is you, Momo."

"Momotarō?"

"Seems it's come to suit you little by little."

Momoko thought so too. "There's nothing I can do about that. I even sit in Dad's old seat at dinnertime." At this point Momoko couldn't remember when she'd started doing it. She hadn't liked the way her father's old seat remained empty at their round dinner table. So she had gradually moved her chair to fill the space, and in doing so she naturally moved into the position where her father used to sit.

Momoko was even the first to be served dinner. And whenever a decision was needed, no matter how big or small, everyone would naturally look to Momoko. When they heard that a typhoon was approaching, Momoko had ordered her mother: "Put fresh batteries in the flashlight." At important ceremonies, it was Momoko who decided how much money to wrap up as a gift. Momoko wouldn't just criticize her little brother and little sister; she came to do the same to her mother too.

"You can mope around all you want, but if he's not coming back, then he's not coming back. If you've got so much spare time, get some sleep or do some work!"

Saying, "Do this! Do that!" had been a habit of her absent father's.

When her little brother passed his university entrance exams, Momoko treated him to dinner alone. She took him to an expensive steakhouse that she had been to once before on company business. She had intended to order a salad for herself and a thick steak for her brother, then drink a toast, and treat him to drinks at a bar after dinner. Even though she didn't have enough money to treat the whole family, she would have felt sorry for Kentarō if she didn't do what her father would have done in a situation like this.

But Kentarō said he didn't want to eat steak. "My stomach feels bad, so a hamburg steak would be better."

He was insistent and unrelenting. Momoko was thinking angrily, *If he just wanted burgers we didn't need to come to an expensive place like this*, when their plates of meat came. The burgers were accompanied by fried eggs, sunny side up. Momoko abruptly remembered something she had seen in the food court of a department store.

A young father who looked like a factory worker was eating hamburg steak with his son, a boy of about junior high school age. When their plates were brought over, the father cut the yolk portion of his fried egg into a square and put it on his son's plate.

"That's the way a father acts."

Momoko cut her egg yolk into a square just like that father and placed it on Kentarō's plate. He was surprised and looked at his sister's face. But then to hide his moistening eyes he looked down, unnerved, and, just like the little boy in the department store, began to eat his double serving of egg yolks silently.

IN FILLING HER FATHER'S role, Momoko had taken to kicking off her shoes in the middle of the foyer. She also felt that her stride had become masculine, with her toes pointed outward.

When she mentioned this to Tsuzuki, he laughed loudly.

"Well, I've never heard of a Momotarō who walks pigeon-toed."

"That would be so weird."

With the momentum of their laughter, their shoulders touched. They had been drinking, and neither Tsuzuki nor Momoko became flustered or pulled away.

TSUZUKI, IN RARE DRUNKEN form that night, performed the "Momotarō" song for Momoko. It was a song her grandmother had sung often when Momoko was in elementary school.

Momotarō, Momotarō
The millet dumplings hanging from your belt
Please give me one

As he sang, Tsuzuki lightly beat time on the back of Momoko's hand, which she had rested on the bar counter. When he came to the "please" part, he placed his hand on hers and left it there for a little while.

Momoko gently tried to pull her hand away.

Tsuzuki moved to the second verse.

I'll give you one; I'll give you one
If you come follow me to conquer demons
I'll give you one

At the end of the song, he moved to hold her hand.

I'll go; I'll go
I'll follow you anywhere
I'll go as your sidekick

Momoko could feel a warmth spreading throughout her body.

Those millet dumplings Tsuzuki wanted, I wonder if he's talking about me. Does he mean that if I give him my millet dumplings he'll be my sidekick and follow me anywhere? Maybe their once-a-month meetings had given rise to something more than just sympathy for the daughter of Tsuzuki's old boss.

In fact, Momoko had started wearing underwear that was fresh out of the laundry on the days when she thought she might get a call from Tsuzuki.

With their nominal "discussions about her father," they had deceived each other about their true feelings. Perhaps their meetings were actually trysts.

In those three years, Momoko had pinched off with her own hand the love that she might have cultivated with others. Pretending that she was already romantically involved, she had passed potential suitors on to other women with a show of nonchalance. When men expressed an interest in her she would set them up with other girls, acting like an expert, and she would even act as an arbitrator if things got complicated. The reason that she had been able to do all of this for so long without feeling crushed was partly because of her family—her mother and siblings—but maybe it was also because of Tsuzuki. Tsuzuki, whom she met once a month and could speak to openly.

Shutting his eyes, Tsuzuki returned again to the first verse and sang in a low voice. Momoko wondered what he would do if she threw herself into his chest and rubbed her forehead against it like she had done when they first visited her father's apartment in Uguisudani. Would he just rub her back like he did then, or would he invite her to some other place?

She had been Momotarō for three years now. She was so tired of it. She wanted to be Momoko and lean against his chest.

Suddenly, she could see the floor plan of a tract house. When she entered, the first room was an eight-tatami-mat dining room and kitchen. Further in, there was the six-mat master bedroom. Then the bath and toilet. On the second floor there were two four-and-a-half-mat rooms for the children. It was Tsuzuki's home. Even the place for the piano, even the location of the propane gas tank he'd been complaining about recently—she could see it as if she had glimpsed it in real life.

This man had a wife and children.

The face of her mother stepping on the pedal of the sewing machine floated before Momoko's eyes. The eldest daughter her mother relied upon more than anyone doing something like that—with a married man of all people—would be like conceding to her runaway father. It would amount to forgiving her father's lover, who had stolen away another woman's husband. Her mother would be hysterical. She would make a scene and put the gas hose from the stove in her mouth, like she did right after her husband left.

Momoko pulled her hand back from Tsuzuki and moved away.

One more year. I have to keep doing this until Kentarō finishes school.

Tsuzuki had been repeating the same verse of the song but now seemed to have remembered the lyrics. He moved on to the next verse.

Then let's keep going, then let's keep going
We'll attack once and destroy them
Crush them; Devil's Island
What fun, what fun
Leaving none standing,
I'll beat them into submission
Take their treasure, here we go
Hurrah, hurrah

My companions, the dog, the monkey,
and the pheasant
Are in high spirits and pull my rickshaw,
here we go

Momoko had a feeling that she would never see a day like that, but Momotarō couldn't just run away and give up.

THE GROUNDS OF THE Hachiman shrine, honoring the Shinto god of war and protector of Japan, were quiet and empty. It was a Sunday afternoon. This seemed like a shrine with some history, but the owners hadn't maintained it well and it was quite dilapidated. In the dirty window of the unmanned shrine office there was a flyer soliciting donations from the parishioners. Momoko had left the house with her mother, who was taking care of some shopping and delivering tailored clothes for her part-time job. Momoko had followed her mother to the shrine, which was on their route.

Her mother chucked a one-hundred-yen coin into the offertory box and clapped her hands loudly. Momoko's mother was a frugal person by nature and had become all the more stingy since her husband left and their income dropped. Momoko, who had assumed that her mother was going to drop in a ten-yen coin, was surprised by the donation.

Her mother prayed for a long time. Momoko too brought her hands together, and she wondered what her mother was praying for. For her husband to come home? Or for misfortune to befall the young woman he was living with?

Momoko had one thing she wanted to apologize for, and the apology was meant for her mother, not for the gods. In secret from both her mother and Tsuzuki, she had gone to see the *oden* shop owned by the woman who lived with her father. Despite having refused to tell her mother its location—"Don't go, ever. If you do, it'll be your loss."—Momoko had developed an intolerable desire to see the face of the woman who had thrown the fate of her father and her family into disarray.

IT WAS A LITTLE shop in an alley behind a train station, and the glass door was fogged up with steam. When Momoko opened the door just a little, an energetic voice greeted her: "Welcome!"

Momoko was taken aback.

The woman was standing behind the counter, so this had to be her. But she looked more like a cleaning lady than a *mama-san*. She appeared older than her years and her face, free of makeup, had a clownish aspect to it. She was wearing a simple cardigan over a dark blouse, and she had tied her hair back tightly with a scarf.

She seemed surprised by the fact that there was a woman by herself at the door.

"I'm sorry but we're full right now," said the hostess.

Men who appeared to be laborers were packed in side-by-side at the counter, which could fit no more than seven people.

"It's fine. Some other time..." As Momoko started to close the glass door with those meaningless words, suddenly the woman said, "Oh!"

The woman's face suddenly became serious. Removing the scarf, she bowed. It was a terribly earnest bow, so deep that her head nearly touched the *oden* pots. She lowered her head as if she knew Momoko.

She wasn't the woman from the Renoir. She wasn't buxom, and she was also no seductress. Momoko went home with the strange feeling that her trust had been profoundly betrayed.

Momoko felt guilty toward her mother for visiting the *oden* shop, but she consoled herself by thinking about her relationship with Tsuzuki. If Momoko had lost her self-control that night, she would have caused her mother more pain than anyone. Tsuzuki had gone home nonchalantly that night, but even if it became a cause for him to distance himself from her, there was nothing she could do about it.

For her family's sake, she couldn't do anything untoward. When she felt beaten down by it all, she would go sit on the bench at Uguisudani Station and calm herself just as she had done in the past. The anger and bitterness she bore toward her father had weathered a lot in the span of three years, but it still had enough power to act as a magic charm.

MOMOKO'S MOTHER CLAPPED HER hands softly twice. She was so much heavier that she looked like a different person than the woman she was three years ago, and she had developed smooth skin, perhaps because of her plumpness. Underneath her bowed head, her kimono collar was speckled by the sunlight filtering through the trees, and she looked strangely feminine.

At one time there had been a gauntness and bitterness that permeated her face and demeanor. For a while Momoko had felt that it was pathetic, even though it was her own mother's face. But in the past six months, in fact, that face had taken on a certain serenity.

"Won't it be good to put an end to this, sign the divorce papers, and start living a new life?" Staring at the hairline at the base of her mother's neck, Momoko thought to herself that she might try out that phrase when her mother was in a good mood.

Momoko didn't know what her mother had wished for, but the one-hundred-yen offering definitely didn't have any effect.

Her little brother Kentarō moved out of the house. He had been complaining about the noise from their mother's sewing machine and going to a friend's house to study for his tests for a while now. They had always assumed the friend was a boy, but it turned out to be a girl. His "all-night study sessions" were in fact sleepovers with her.

Their mother asked him, "Can't you wait until you graduate?"

His retort was, "You should be glad. This way you don't have to pay for my food."

He left the house carrying only his books and a change of clothes.

Momoko was so angry that her body trembled. She ambushed him in front of one of the classrooms at his school and then grabbed him and practically dragged him to a restaurant in front of the school's entrance. It wasn't mealtime, so the place was empty.

When the waitress came to take their order, Momoko said, "Two hamburg steaks, please. With fried eggs on top." Her eyes met Kentarō's.

Instead of asking Kentarō if he had forgotten about that day, Momoko wanted to shove the actual thing in front of him. *Not wearing what you want to wear, abandoning love, trying to fill your father's shoes for three years, what do you think of that?* Momoko wanted to scream it.

The burgers and the accompanying eggs arrived. Kentarō took his knife and, just like his older sister did two and a half years ago, cut the yolk into a square, putting it on Momoko's plate.

"You can't just give it back," said Momoko.

Kentarō began to silently cut his burger into small pieces.

"I'm not trying to pin you down with a debt of gratitude for what I've done. I'm not asking you to pay back the tuition I've paid for you. I'm all right myself, but I want to tell you that I feel bad for Mom."

"Oh yeah?"

"What do you mean by 'oh yeah?' You don't feel sorry for her?"

Kentarō put down his fork and looked at his sister's face.

"I think you'd be better off if you used the time you spend worrying about others to think about yourself."

"What do you mean?"

"Everyone's getting by all right."

To Kentarō's surprise, while waiting to meet someone in front of the statue of Hachiko in Shibuya, he had spotted their mother also in front of the statue, apparently waiting for someone herself. Kentarō was even more surprised when their father appeared. Their father led the way wordlessly, starting off toward the nearby upward slope of Dōgenzaka. Their mother followed two or three steps behind.

"I felt bad about following them, but I did. Then . . ."

Kentarō hesitated and looked down.

The two of them had gone into a love hotel.

"When was this?"

"About six months ago, I guess."

Momoko felt the air rush from her body as if she were a balloon that had been poked with a needle.

MOMOKO DASHED INTO A beauty parlor and had her hair cut. Unwilling to spare the cost of having her hair set, she hadn't even had a perm in the past three years. Her hair had grown until it was about shoulder-length. There was no way she could calm herself down if she didn't do something, and she had no idea what would come out of her mouth if she confronted her mother in this state.

Lying on her back looking up and having her hair washed, Momoko was filled with anger again. Come to think of it, she remembered something from six months ago. It was then that Momoko's mother had come to be more mindful of her appearance, and she would leave the house saying that other divorcees working part-time jobs wanted her advice about their circumstances.

In fact, she had been meeting Momoko's father outside. She had become more womanly than when he was in the house. So wasn't Momoko's mother a mistress herself? What had Momoko being doing these past three years?

Life is a one-two punch. The words were Kiyoko Suizenji's.

Despite being a woman, Momoko had taken on fatherly pretensions, acted like a commanding officer, given orders. It was all so absurd that it brought tears to her eyes. For three years she had sealed up her true feelings as a woman and donned armor on both her body and her heart.

A cracked walnut
Inside that cracked walnut
Is an unused room

She had forgotten when and where she had seen it, but Momoko remembered having read that haiku. If she remembered correctly, the author was unknown. But this poem had stuck in a corner of her mind.

Her dependence on others and her jealousy were twice as strong as an average person's, but she went around acting as if she hadn't been born with those traits. And on the other side of a thin membrane, her true feelings, feelings that not even she had noticed, were alive and well. Even if she did become aware of them now, was it too late? Maybe the time for fruition had passed. Wrapped in astringent coating, the white, oily walnut was the hairline at the base of her mother's neck.

If her father hadn't left the house, her mother surely would have finished her life as a tense, bony woman. That plump mother who happily went out to meet her husband had stepped for the first time into a previously unused room.

THE STYLIST WAS CUTTING Momoko's wet hair. Momoko went ahead and had the woman shear it off below her ears. Her bobbed hair, sticking close to her skin, was exactly like the hair on Momotarō in a picture book she had seen as a child.

Geta

KŌICHIRŌ KAKIZAKI HAD A habit of mentally writing his diary entry every day before the day's end, though it wasn't clear whether this was a matter of punctiliousness or impatience.

It would go like this: "Day X, Month X: Ōsawa's been out because he's in mourning, but he came in to work today. There's an old saying that if there's an elderly person in the family, the family should be prepared for a funeral and keep their effects in order. After some idle chat, Ōsawa called me into the hallway. Turned out that the cash, that crucial item, wasn't in the gift envelope I gave him at the funeral."

Kōichirō worked for an art publishing company with less than fifty employees. The company was located near Yotsuya Station in a small, old building, using the first floor for the sales department and the second for the editorial department. It was an established company in the industry, with extravagant expense policies that had strong support among the company's client base.

Kōichirō worked on the monthly art magazine desk. Ōsawa had been behind him in college. He had entered during the year when Kōichirō graduated, so he would be thirty-five or thirty-six now. For the past week he had been in mourning for his late father, and today was his first day back in the office. He went around to the employees who had helped with the wake and the funeral, saying, "I was really embarrassed," and bowing his head.

"If I'd known he was going to up and die all of a sudden, I would have cleaned up my place ahead of time. My wife is really messy, so when you open our closets, the floor cushions just fall out, and our laundry is just stuffed in there," Ōsawa joked in his characteristically cheerful voice.

Apparently this had actually happened, to judge by the glances and snickers that some of the women in the office were exchanging.

Kōichirō had seen his own father off seven years earlier. When the undertaker moved a bookshelf to make room for the altar in their house, an *abunae*, a sexually graphic woodblock print, had fallen onto the tatami mats from its hiding place behind the bookshelf. It was actually work-related, a high-quality piece by a famous artist, but it still would have caused trouble if the children had caught sight of it.

Kōichirō remembered breaking out into a cold sweat at that time, and now he responded to Ōsawa with a measure of kindness in his tone: "A funeral is just like surrendering a castle. You can't complain no matter what anyone opens up."

Holding a pipe in his mouth, their editor-in-chief, Kurosu, joined the conversation. "That's no cause for embarrassment."

"I'm sure you've heard this story before," said Kurosu, launching into an anecdote about an employee of a certain newspaper company. There was no funeral involved, but the employee wasn't feeling well at work, so a coworker walked him home from the office. Once they got to the house, the coworker saw something he shouldn't have. The teacups, dishes, spoons—all of them were from the company cafeteria. Even the slippers were from the night-duty room.

Kurosu's nickname was "the Aesthete." He was the son of the president of the company, and, maybe because he had wanted to be an art critic in his younger days, he absolutely despised anything unsightly or ugly.

Kurosu laughed at the story along with the other employees, but the Aesthete's laugh had a colder element than other people's.

When the joking was over, the employees started their work, and Ōsawa poked Kōichirō in the elbow. His eyes invited Kōichirō to follow him, hinting that he had something to talk to Kōichirō about. He walked out into the hallway one step ahead of Kōichirō. The editorial department was one big room without dividers, so there was no place of refuge. There was nothing to do but hold private conversations in a nearby coffee shop or right there in the hallway.

Ōsawa stood in front of the nearest men's bathroom just off the corridor. Looking embarrassed and stammering, he broached the subject: "So, there wasn't any money in your condolence envelope."

The scene came to Kōichirō's mind. He had written the address on the envelope, and when the time came to insert the money, he realized he didn't have any crisp ten-thousand-yen bills. His seventy-year-old mother, Takie, overheard him scolding his wife, Naoko, for forgetting to at least prepare some crisp bills.

"One is enough, I suppose," said Takie, loosening her kimono sash. Pulling a fresh bill out of a pocket inside the sash, she continued, "Whether it's a wedding or a funeral, the cost is no small matter. We're lucky we don't have a big family."

It was perhaps the considerable intensity with which she spoke that caused her to suffer a fit right then. She had chronic paroxysmal tachycardia, which caused her heartbeat to speed up drastically for short periods. She crouched down on the floor. The spasm was soon over, but the commotion threw everything into disarray and Kōichirō forgot to put the critical money in the envelope.

Ōsawa was embarrassed, but Kōichirō felt worse.

"Thanks for telling me." He extended a ten-thousand-yen bill to Ōsawa, worrying that it was a bit wrinkled. Ōsawa joked lightly by slicing the air three times to thank the gods and put the bill in his pocket.

"I'll finish the mourning period soon, so let's do a bit of this." Ōsawa gestured lining up some mah-jongg tiles. "I'll let you know, so please come and win back your money."

"You don't need to say that right to my face."

They disguised their mutual unease through these jokes.

Kōichirō's nickname was "Mah-jongg Tile." His jaw and face were both square.

Since he was already out in the hallway, he went to relieve himself in the bathroom. He added a new line to the diary he was keeping in his head, with words scripted in characters as square as his face. "Hugely embarrassed. Had ten thousand yen taken from me."

THE REST OF THE day passed as usual.

Whenever Kōichirō's glance met Ōsawa's, he was bothered by Ōsawa's embarrassed and apologetic expression. Kōichirō was also irritated by the Aesthete's pretentious comments, as well as the way in which the young, supplicating Miyake responded to the editor-in-chief with flattery. That was how the day passed until dusk.

A deadline was fast approaching. After seeing off the editor-in-chief to a roundtable discussion about the next issue, the remaining editorial employees ordered dinner because they were working overtime, and then they had to get back to work.

"He's here. He's here."

The women in the office rose from their seats to prepare the tea.

The *tock tock* sound of wooden geta sandals rose up the stairwell and came through the hallway. It was the delivery boy from Shinyōken. The noise of his sandals resounded even inside the editing room, probably because the building was made of undressed concrete. The sneakers that were popular these days would have been easier on a delivery boy's feet, but occasionally there were delivery boys who would come wearing tall geta like these, made from magnolia wood, their steps resounding throughout the building. Maybe they wore the geta because the restaurant's kitchen floor was wet, or maybe it was just that some of the restaurant workers were a little pretentious.

They had been seeing a lot of the Shinyōken delivery boy lately. He was a chunky young man. Kōichirō couldn't once remember hearing him say "Thanks for your frequent business" or "Sorry to have kept you waiting," as was customary. But that was probably because he would mumble the words, with a demeanor that was more melancholy than shy.

The delivery boy would not go right back to the restaurant after he finished dishing out the dumplings and fried rice. He would procrastinate, peeking at the layout forms and touching the color samples, while still remaining mindful of his greasy hands.

Shinyōken was a dingy restaurant, but it was doing well. If he went back to the store he would surely have to deliver another order. He was probably just taking a break now that he was out of the restaurant for a bit.

He's lazy despite his youth, thought Kōichirō. But that particular evening wasn't an opportunity for the delivery boy to relax. Apparently he had mixed up the order, and Miyake ordered him to "Go back and fix this!"

Miyake had always dined with the editor-in-chief when he was attending one of the roundtable discussions, but for about a month now a newly arrived female employee had been beating Miyake at his own game. Now, he seemed to be taking out his frustration on the delivery boy.

It must have been raining that evening, because the delivery boy's hair and shoulders were wet, even though Shinyōken was only two streets behind the office.

A bit roughly, Kōichirō exchanged Miyake's meal for his own. "It's just one meal, so does it really matter what you eat? You're not going to die because your sweet-and-sour pork turned into *gomoku soba*."

Miyake didn't press the matter further.

The delivery boy bowed his head toward Kōichirō and left, but his geta made noise as he returned once more.

Standing behind Kōichirō as he split his take-out

chopsticks, the boy said, "Sorry, do you have a minute?" He asked Kōichirō to come into the hallway with him.

He was standing in front of the men's bathroom.

Cutting-edge architecture ages faster than a face. The bare concrete office building that had been pictured in an architecture magazine around the time that Kōichirō started at the company was now speckled with conspicuous gray blotches, and on rainy days it smelled like a wet rag.

No matter the circumstances, to be summoned to the same place twice in one day was strange. Kōichirō had decided that the delivery boy was surely going to thank him, but as he approached, he felt uneasy when he noticed that the boy's breathing was strangely rough.

I'll tell him not to worry about it, to feel better, and clap him on the shoulder, thought Kōichirō. Kōichirō started to say the words, but then the boy began to speak with a voice that seemed to be caught in his throat, "Mister, your... Mister, isn't your father's name Kōtarō Kakizaki?"

"Well, yeah. Do you know him?"

The boy's nasal breathing became even rougher.

"I'm his son." Neither laughing nor crying, with his mouth open, he stared up at Kōichirō.

Even wearing the magnolia wood geta, he was still shorter than Kōichirō.

LATE THAT EVENING, KŌICHIRŌ listened to the boy's story at a snack bar in the neighborhood. He was twenty. When he heard that the boy's name was Kōji Matsuura, Kōichirō felt once again like his head had been battered.

His father, whom Kōichirō had always thought

of as a strait-laced man, had kept a mistress. He had had an illegitimate child. Kōichirō had always thought of himself as an only child, but in fact he had a brother. Moreover, even though his father hadn't acknowledged the child, he had chosen for the boy a name with the same "kō" character used in Kōichirō's name.

Kōji said that when his mother was young, she had waitressed in a small restaurant in the Ueno district of Tokyo. Kōichirō's father, who was employed at a semi-governmental organization involved in public works, had apparently formed a romantic bond with her in that part of town.

After Kōji was born, he was quickly sent to a distant relative's house as a foster child, so he had absolutely no memory of his father. His mother fell ill and died when he was in junior high school. When Kōji went to visit his mother in the hospital, carrying his schoolbag, she made him take out his Japanese language textbook and write "Kōtarō Kakizaki" on the first page.

Next to that she made him write Kōichirō, and told him that Kōichirō was his older brother. Unlike Kōji, Kōichirō was apparently a smart guy. When she began to explain that Kōichirō was working at a publishing company in Yotsuya, the nurse came in and asked Kōji to leave. His mom wasn't able to speak at all after that, and soon afterward she died.

"When I was looking for a job, y'know, I looked in the Yotsuya area. I guess, y'know, I was thinking about what she said."

Kōji apparently had a habit of saying "y'know."

"I volunteered to do takeout deliveries for publishing companies, but I never thought I would find you. When I heard the name 'Kakizaki,' it was hard for me to breathe. I thought that you, Mister, also had your own reputation to worry about."

In a muffled voice, Kōji said, "I told myself that I definitely shouldn't say anything and kept myself in check, but I just couldn't keep it in any longer."

So apparently that was why Kōji would procrastinate after making his deliveries instead of heading straight back to the restaurant.

"Y'know, our faces look alike too."

Kōichirō had noticed it as well. Kōji also had a square, sharp-jawed face.

"My nickname is 'Geta.'"

"Mine is 'Tile.' As in 'mah-jongg tile.'"

The two of them laughed for the first time.

Maybe it was Kōichirō's imagination, but even their laughs seemed similar.

"Now that you mention it, your skin is whiter than mine, like a mah-jongg tile."

"Wait a minute. I've also been called 'Geta.' When I was in junior high I was Geta."

There was a pause in their conversation.

Kōichirō recalled the contours of his dead father's appearance. He wondered what his father's nickname had been. Might Kōji, sitting next to him and silently fiddling with his beer glass, be wondering the same thing?

"Geta—" Kōji looked up at Kōichirō. "Y'know, geta come in pairs."

Kōichirō let out a big laugh, but at the same time, he thought that this was a very weighty joke. Instead of saying, "I'm your little brother. I'm your sibling," Kōji had said that the two of them were a pair of geta.

As he poured beer for Kōji, Kōichirō asked about his brother's salary. As he did so, Kōichirō was surprised at himself when he deftly picked up the wallet that had popped out of the back pocket of Kōji's jeans and examined it. He generally had good manners, and he had never done anything like that to his wife Naoko or his mother. Wasn't this surely a brotherly mannerism?

The contents of Kōji's wallet were pathetic. Kōichirō couldn't return it like that, so he put a ten-thousand-yen bill inside. Kōji watched silently, but bowed his head with a jerk as though he had just broken his neck.

THE NEXT DAY WAS Sunday. In part because it was the day after his deadline, Kōichirō spent all day idling about inside the house, even more taciturn than usual.

Naoko cut up a small watermelon for an afternoon snack. She sliced it through the center into six pieces, and each member of the five-person family—Kōichirō, Naoko, their two children, and his mother—took a slice and ate it.

Naoko saw the one slice left on the tray and said, "There's always one piece left over. It's really tough to cut a melon for a family of five."

Hearing this, Kōichirō was a little pained. He wanted to say, "Well, he might not be part of our family, but there is one person who could eat this leftover red slice and it wouldn't be that strange."

"THE YOUNG DELIVERY BOY from Shinyōken turned out to be my brother by a different mother; it was earth-shattering. For the time being, I gave him ten thousand yen as spending money." In reality, Kōichirō probably should have written as much in his diary yesterday, but of course he couldn't. From that day forward his diary was just empty white paper. He understood well that the ultimate truth was something he couldn't put in writing.

"I'LL CONTACT YOU SOON."

Kōji had said these words at the intersection in front of the train station before they went their separate ways. When Kōichirō raised his hand, said, "See you," and started to walk away, Kōji mumbled, "Is it all right if I call you my brother?"

Kōichirō couldn't muster a response at that moment. Then he said "yeah" in an inaudible voice that felt like a low growl.

Kōji, apparently getting the message, said, "Yeah, it's still early for that." Embarrassed, he spoke the words as if he were talking to himself. His expression was that of a worldly-wise man, older than his years, and he ran off across the black, rain-soaked pavement.

"Hey, wait!" Kōichirō called to stop him.

If Kōichirō could have embraced his brother and said, "I'm sure you've suffered. If anything happens, come to my place," how moving would that have been for Kōji? Kōichirō himself would also surely have been satisfied. He understood as much, but he couldn't say those words.

In part, he was embarrassed. Part of it was also his awkward shyness. And he couldn't bear to explain this to his mother.

Her deceased husband had been overly critical, but he had never caused her any grief with other women. To tell the old woman who found encouragement in life by repeating the phrase "There aren't any women as happy as me"—to tell her that her dead husband had betrayed her twenty years ago—would probably give her a heart attack, if it didn't kill her outright.

Kōichirō explained that to Kōji. He was understanding.

"It's too sudden for her. And she's not mentally prepared for this." Kōichirō said that his office would probably keep ordering takeout from Shinyōken, and to keep their blood relationship a secret between the two of them for now.

When Kōichirō looked at Kōji, he felt longing and pity on one hand, and repugnance on the other.

His face is square like mine. Having been passed around from house to house since he was young, Kōji was sensitive to people's expressions.

Kōji kept calling Kōichirō "Mister" and saying, "y'know, y'know." These habits, combined with his job as a delivery boy for a Chinese restaurant, made him the kind of person who would be most shunned by the aesthete Kurosu. If Kurosu knew that Kōichirō was that boy's brother, Kurosu would ostracize him just for that. Kurosu was that kind of man.

Kōichirō complained about this and that at the office, but he didn't want to become a laughingstock or an outcast within the company he had worked at for seventeen years.

And there was one more thing.

Although Kōji had spoken to Kōichirō as he might have spoken to family, his word choice and the quickness with which his tone had become familiar were a little frightening to Kōichirō.

At first, Kōji had been pretty polite, but by the time they had parted ways that first evening, he had become much more casual. One of these days, "Mister" would become "Bro."

And—

When Kōichirō tried to think of how things might develop from there, his head ached and felt heavy.

JUST HEARING "SHINYŌKEN" WAS enough to make Kōichirō uneasy.

Even when there wasn't any overtime work, if it was raining or nasty out, the women in the office didn't want to leave and would order takeout. Kōji would come by just as though he'd been waiting for the order. Maybe it was only Kōichirō's imagination, but even the sound of Kōji's geta coming up the stairs seemed to be full of self-confidence.

Kōji's timid attitude disappeared little by little. He started calling the editorial department employees by their names. Sometimes at night he would stand by the desks and pass his eyes leisurely over the evening paper, wooden carrying-box in hand, before going back to the restaurant.

Kōichirō felt guilty for not introducing him to everybody and found it difficult to tell Kōji not to take things any further than this.

Kōichirō also bumped into Kōji in front of a train station at one point. A silver blood-donation van was parked nearby.

Suddenly, Kōji said, "Hey, I think I'll give blood." In a lower voice, he added, "Why don't we do it together?"

The truth was that Kōichirō didn't feel like it. Lined up on the bed, lined up next to Kōji, the needle piercing his arm, having two hundred milliliters of blood drawn out. The two men's blood would meet for the first time and be intermixed in the glass container, and then enter the body of some unknown person.

Whether he had thought it through that far or not, it was a painful concept for Kōichirō at any rate. And it wasn't part of his brotherly duties.

"If you don't do it, Mister, then I won't either," said Kōji as he stopped himself.

This time too, it wasn't until after the men had parted ways that Kōichirō thought there was something touching about Kōji going so far out of a desire to confirm that they were blood relatives.

"HONEY, WHAT ARE YOU doing in there?" Naoko asked, and Kōichirō was at a loss.

On Sunday morning, after urging his family to go out, he had entered the storage room and was rummaging around. Kōji had asked him for one article of clothing, any article, that their father had worn.

However, perhaps as a form of punishment for never helping with the housecleaning, Kōichirō couldn't even guess where anything was put away. On the right side of some dusty clothing boxes piled together, he saw "husband's brown business suit and trousers" written in his mother's handwriting.

Thinking he'd found what he needed, Kōichirō unfastened the string on the box and removed the cover, getting dust all over his hands. But inside there were only an old water pillow, ice pack, and bath towel. His search wasn't going anywhere.

Kōichirō's family discovered him while he was bumbling around. He tried to smooth things over with Naoko by telling her he had suddenly remembered a fishing tackle he had used quite some time ago and so now he was looking for it. But Naoko peered into his eyes with an expression of doubt the way she did when she sensed something was a little off and said, "This is the most formative time for our kids, you know. Please don't act like a fool."

I'm not the one acting the fool. That was my dad. Kōichirō couldn't say the words, and he was at his wits' end in the storage room, dust floating in the air.

KŌJI WAS A LIVE-IN employee. There were seven male employees at Shinyōken, and four of them lived in company housing. Though they called it a "dorm," it was a dilapidated two-story building nearby that they rented cheaply, comprised of only a shabby kitchen and two rooms. Each of the rooms, barely one hundred and twenty-five square feet each, was shared by two of the housemates.

"I want you to see where I live," Kōji had said. Kōichirō had peeked inside. The startling vulgarity and squalidness of this all-male household was quite something.

There were posters of singers and nude pictures not only next to the bed but also all around, up to the ceiling. There was a bag of partially eaten snack food right by the bed, and above it there was a pair of multicolored striped underpants airing out on a round drying rack that swayed back and forth.

Round drying racks seemed popular in this dorm; there were two in each room, swaying above the beds.

On the days they had off from work, the four men would add to the overflowing chaos of the dorm by listening to their stereo with the volume turned up very high.

In showing this to Kōichirō, had Kōji wanted to reveal to his brother his longstanding loneliness, or his poverty? Whichever it was, Kōichirō soon found himself meeting Kōji's girlfriend, as if everything had happened in one sequence.

Her name was Kimiko and she worked at a snack bar that Kōji frequented. She was young, but she put on her makeup like a middle-aged woman, and her skin looked worn beyond its years. She wasn't bad-looking, but there was a problem with her mouth; there was some lipstick on her teeth, probably because they were crooked and protruding.

Compared to Kōji's enthusiasm, the woman didn't seem to care much about him.

Kimiko called Kōichirō "brother."

From far away, Kōichirō felt something invisible approaching him with a certain steadiness. Before he realized what was happening, he had lost control of his legs. He was drowning. He thought he would have to draw the line there, but when push came to shove he couldn't refuse Kōji.

KŌJI HAD COME WITH a delivery. Standing behind Kōichirō, as he peeked at the color samples, he had asked with his eyes, "Could I have just a moment?" and stepped out ahead of Kōichirō.

There was something forceful about the *tock tock* sound of his geta.

Kōichirō went into the hallway as if he were getting up to use the bathroom. Kōji was waiting for him in the place where he had first asked the name of Kōichirō's father.

Standing in front of the speckled, pale gray concrete walls, with Kōji's square face staring at him, part of Kōichirō couldn't resist. By the time he came to himself, he had already said, "Yeah."

The seventh anniversary of his father's death was drawing near.

By the time Kōichirō realized what was happening, he had already said to Kōji, "Our family burial ground is at Tama Cemetery."

THE ANNIVERSARY FELL ON a Sunday, but Kōichirō told Kōji to meet him at seven o'clock at Koganei Station. Using the excuse of a business-related game of golf, he told Kōji that they had to visit their father's grave at that early hour or they wouldn't be able to do it together.

Kōji had arrived before him and was waiting. He was in rare form, in a black business suit, and was carrying a long, slender box.

On the way to the cemetery, they came across an elementary school preparing for an athletics festival.

Where did you go to elementary school?

Were you a fast runner, were you good at races?

Did you ever get hurt?

Who came to cheer you on at the festivals?

Kōichirō was better off not asking these questions. If he did, he would be walking step by step into a quagmire. He knew this, but as they walked side by side down the tree-lined avenue of the cemetery, he couldn't stop himself from inquiring.

"The Kakizaki Family Gravesite," as it was labeled, seemed horribly small, perhaps because it was near the grave of an elder statesman from the Meiji era.

Kōji took the cork out of a two-liter bottle he had brought with him and poured some of its contents onto the gravestone. Maybe he had heard from his deceased mother that their father liked sake.

Kōichirō was a little uneasy. Two hours later he would be bringing his mother, his wife, and his kids here to visit the grave. It would be a problem if it smelled of liquor then.

But the weather was nice and the alcohol would probably evaporate quickly. And if it did smell, Kōichirō could feign ignorance and claim that some friend of his father's had probably come, and that would be the end of it.

Kōji abruptly stopped pouring from the bottle and pushed it toward Kōichirō. There were three centimeters of alcohol left at the bottom.

He thought that Kōji was telling him to pour some on the gravestone, but Kōji wiped the mouth of the bottle with his palm and said, "You first, Mister."

Apparently his intention was to exchange drinks in front of their father's grave.

Part of Kōichirō was embarrassed, either because the gesture was so dramatic or, perhaps, because it was so forced. But the early autumn morning gave a smooth feel to his skin, and that was pleasant.

When Kōichirō heard the gentle chirping of a small bird, he thought that it would be tiresome to bring up his difference of opinion on something so inconsequential.

"I'll go after you, Mister," said Kōji again.

Kōichirō snatched the bottle away from him violently.

"I've been meaning to say this: stop calling me 'Mister'!" As soon as he'd said that, Kōichirō took a swig and thrust the bottle at Kōji.

In a small voice, Kōji muttered, "my brother."

"And one more thing. Stop saying 'y'know'!"

Kōji nodded his head so low he looked like he was about to topple over. He drank the rest of the sake in a single gulp.

KŌICHIRŌ AND KŌJI SPLIT up at Koganei Station. Kōichirō hurried home and then Naoko drove the family to the cemetery. They could hear the swelling sounds of marching rhythms and starting pistol shots from the speakers at the elementary school where earlier in the morning the athletics festival had been setting up.

As Kōichirō supported Takie, whose legs and lower back had recently become very weak, they walked between the tombstones to the gravesite.

Kōichirō was worried about the smell of sake, but the alcohol had drifted away on the wind. Strangely enough, however, there were seven or eight large black flies gathered on the gravestone. Perhaps the evaporated sake had left a sweet residue.

He was reminded of his father, who had hated flies and mosquitoes and would often chase them with a flyswatter while having his evening drink.

His father would be upset if he didn't get the insect in one shot. In fact, he would grumble even if he did get it in one blow but the fly didn't drop to the ground with its body intact. He must have hated the sight of a fly or mosquito that he had hit with too much force and crushed.

"Out of sight, out of mind. The way your father has others do the bad jobs that he could do himself, that's what I call selfishness." Takie used to say things like that behind her husband's back.

Naoko put some flowers on the grave, and Kōichirō used a lighter to ignite the bundle of incense sticks that his mother had carried to the gravesite.

The family of five lined up in front of the tomb just as they always did. Takie poked Kōichirō in the side.

"Is that someone you know?"

It was Kōji. The man standing a short distance away and looking toward them was the same Kōji he had parted with a short while ago at Koganei Station.

"Nope, I don't know him. He's probably waiting for someone," Kōichirō answered nonchalantly and clasped his hands. But he was so angry that his body was shaking.

He was angry at Kōji, Kōji who had waited here, who had realized that his work-related game of golf was a lie, who had expected that Kōichirō would surely be coming here with his family.

He was also angry with his father, the man who had put up a façade of being strait-laced but had conceived a child with another woman and then abandoned both the woman and the child.

Kōichirō's anger also began to boil at his old mother, who was blind to her husband's faults and had believed that this sort of thing wouldn't be a problem when it came to her husband, and her husband alone.

In this world, things aren't that perfect. Dad was a man of flesh and blood. And the person standing over there is my little brother. Kōichirō wanted to tell her that.

He also wanted to say it to his son and daughter who were clasping their hands perfunctorily. *You have somebody to thank for being able to act impertinent. Look at that man standing over there.* Even the fact that his son's jaw was square like Kōji's was provoking.

"The air is really nice here, isn't it?"

He also wanted to say it to his wife, who was yawning softly. Don't you think that your husband's been acting strange lately? Our envelope to

Ōsawa was missing that ten-thousand-yen bill and you were flustered and apologized, but there's a bigger issue going on here.

Getting older as he was, Kōichirō's anger was endless. He was angry most of all with himself, struggling again and again to carry this enormous burden that he couldn't bear alone, his illegitimate brother. He waved his hand around to chase away the black flies that were swarming around his face and buzzing impudently.

SITTING NEXT TO HIM, Ōsawa said, "Kōichirō, phone call." And then, as Ōsawa handed over the receiver to Kōichirō, he mouthed, "A woman."

This happened two or three days after Kōichirō's visit to the cemetery.

He said, "This is Kōichirō," and after a moment a relaxed woman's voice on the other end said, "This is his big brother?" Her tone was overly familiar.

It was Kimiko, Kōji's girlfriend. She said she wanted to get Kōichirō's advice.

He listened to her story at a nearby snack bar during his lunch break. Apparently, there was a stand-and-eat soba shop up for sale near Shinōkubo Station on the Chūo train line. Kōji had been saying that if his elder brother lent them the money, then he and Kimiko could turn the store into a Chinese soba and dumpling shop. It seemed like she would be willing to marry Kōji if they opened up the shop.

Kōichirō began to feel a hot mass rising in the pit of his stomach again.

"I don't know what Kōji told you, but I'm nothing more than a businessman at a small-scale publishing company. I'm doing everything I can to pay off the loans on my house, and there's no way I could give you financial support, nor would I want to. We do have something of a connection, so I'm not saying I won't help you at all, but you have to live your own lives." When he came to himself, he realized that his tone was vehement.

Kimiko sucked on her straw through her lipstick-specked teeth.

Ōsawa was in a distant seat, looking at them. After Kimiko got up to leave, Kōichirō wondered what kind of relationship an unrelated observer would have guessed they had with each other.

EVEN KŌICHIRŌ HIMSELF REALIZED that he was being stubborn. When the female employees in the office asked if they should get food from Shinyōken while they worked overtime, he would respond, "That's really just more of the same. Isn't there a place we haven't tried yet?" Part of him just didn't want to see Kōji's face again.

About a week or less had passed when Kōji came by. The restaurant had raised its prices and he walked in to deliver the new menus to the editorial department. He placed one behind Kōichirō's seat and said, "Please consider ordering from us." Then he nudged Kōichirō in the back. It seemed to be a signal that he would be waiting for Kōichirō in the hall.

Kōichirō understood but he didn't go. Probably five minutes passed. The geta sounded a familiar *tock tock*, and Kōji came back.

"Oh, it's the guy from Shinyōken. Did you forget something?" asked one of the female employees.

Without answering her question, Kōji went to stand behind Kōichirō again.

"Brother." Kōji's voice was low, but Kōichirō

heard it clearly. He was struck with horror that Ōsawa, sitting next to him and editing an article, might also have heard.

Kōichirō went into the hallway after Kōji. The bad weather had persisted, and the gray concrete walls of the hallway smelled like a rotten rag.

Kōichirō said it flat out: "If you're not discreet, it's going to cause serious problems for me."

"You're wrong if you think you're the only injured party here. Think about it from my side. Both my mother and I could call ourselves victims." Kōji's teary eyes returned Kōichirō's glare.

The bathroom door opened with a *plunk*, and Kurosu appeared, shaking water off his hands. The gesture was somewhat incongruous with his nickname. But then he asked Kōichirō, "What's happening here?" and it was Kōichirō's turn to get agitated. He couldn't very well have Kurosu saying that he had made the ramen shop delivery boy cry in the hallway.

"This is only going to be a one-item order, but please do it for me," said Kōichirō. Even he didn't know what the "it" was, but in this situation he could find no other way out.

Kōji returned with an order of roast pork ramen in no time. With a hard expression, he stood behind Kōichirō and put the ramen on Kōichirō's desk with a thud. The broth splattered grandly onto a manuscript. The gesture was clearly intentional.

At that point, Kōichirō could barely contain his explosive anger any longer. He was about to give Kōji a good beating and tell him that he was pushing way too far, counting too much on Kōichirō's indulgence.

Kōichirō's hand just about flew out at Kōji, but he held himself back. *He probably wants me to smack him. If I do it here, I'll have to look after this guy my whole life.* Kōichirō just barely managed to control himself, and Kōji repeatedly mumbled some vague words of apology and went back to the restaurant, his geta *tock-tock*ing.

KŌICHIRŌ WAS AT A loss when his wife said stiffly, "It seems like you're trying to hide something."

Initially he was alarmed, but Naoko didn't suspect anything about Kōji. Kōichirō was relieved to find out she was worried that he was being unfaithful to her.

Over this past half year, whenever he had had free time, he had spent it with Kōji. He hadn't been spending time with his family on Sundays, and he hadn't invited Ōsawa and the rest of his colleagues to play mah-jongg because he was afraid of letting word about Kōji slip out. He hadn't noticed it himself, but there must have been moments when he was lost in thought or let out an unfamiliar sigh.

"People say that this kind of thing happens every other generation. Your grandfather was a soft man, and your father was a straight shooter, so Naoko has to keep an eye on you." Takie had said this to them casually, in blissful ignorance.

Kōichirō decided to let her hang onto her illusions. *It's not like I have to keep this secret for another thirty or fifty years. As long as word of Kōji doesn't reach her ears before she dies, she can at least maintain the happiness of an ordinary woman until she passes away.*

As he was thinking this, Kōichirō realized that somewhere in his feelings was a wish for his mother's death. Might she be able to die before the Kōji affair became public? Children can be so cruel sometimes.

ONE DAY, COMPLETELY OUT of the blue, Kōichirō's company went bankrupt. Some people said that Kurosu's sense of aesthetics had destroyed the company. Kōji came to the office as they were being simultaneously confronted by creditors and a labor union, a time when everything was in frantic disarray.

As usual, Kōji called Kōichirō into the hallway. He extended toward Kōichirō an envelope on which he had written "A Farewell Gift" in a crude hand. Inside was a ten-thousand-yen bill.

Kōichirō sliced the air in gratitude, accepting it, and said, "Thanks."

"When you find a new job—"

"—I'll call Shinyōken."

Kōji nodded. And then he let out a small exclamation: "Ah! Our fingernails are the same shape."

Now that he mentioned it, both Kōichirō's and Kōji's fingernails were square and stubby.

TWO MONTHS HAD PASSED since that day. Kōichirō came to long for that face, the face that he had found repugnant when it was actually near him, for Kōji's short height, exaggerated by his tall geta, for his unattractive appearance, for Koji's calculating aspect hidden behind timidity. He thought nostalgically of Kōji's way of life, like a rising tide moving steadily up the shore, like an inchworm that made no sound and spoke no words and yet had already arrived by the time one became conscious of its presence. Once they were separated, he found himself missing Kōji.

He began to think of Kōji as an irreplaceable brother. The shape of Kōji's square fingernails, covered in grease, came into his mind.

CLOSE TO THE END of the year, Kōichirō finally found work. It was at a design company in a small building in Sotokanda.

Kōichirō knew that he should put in a call to Shinyōken, but feeling as though this time had been a long vacation from his responsibilities to Kōji, he wanted to keep his brother in the dark for a little longer.

The end of the year was drawing near, so Kōichirō had overtime work even though he was new to the company. Despite being older, he was still a first-year employee, and the women in the office who had seniority over him took charge of ordering food for the employees working overtime.

He heard the sound from the hall while he was working on a layout. The *tock tock* of geta. Apparently, the food was here. He was startled; geta were rare these days.

Maybe it's him.

Had Kōji inquired at Kōichirō's old office as they were settling their affairs and determined the location of his new office? Just as he had discovered Kōichirō before while knowing only that Kōichirō worked in Yotsuya?

I have nothing to worry about. He's not the only delivery boy who wears geta.

Tock tock.

Soon the door opened.

Spring Has Come

PERHAPS THERE WAS SOMETHING in the blackness of the coffee that made women put on airs. Or maybe it was the café, built out of glass and metal piping that had a silvery sparkle. Whichever it was, Naoko realized that she was embellishing things.

"My father works in P.R."

"Like at an advertising company?"

Ryūichi Kazami sat across from her. His long fingers reached into his pack of Cabin cigarettes, extracted one, and drew it to his mouth.

"He manages the company together with a good friend from college."

"Oh, so he's an executive?"

Instead of answering, Naoko plucked a match from one of the café's matchbooks and lit it. She wasn't used to the gesture, so she fumbled and came dangerously close to burning the tip of her finger.

"Ouch!"

She didn't make it to the ashtray, and the cinders of the match fell into Kazami's water glass with a sizzle.

"Sorry about that."

Naoko started to raise her hand to request another glass of water but Kazami smiled at her. Then he reached out silently and took a sip from the glass she'd been drinking from. She could feel the blood rising in her cheeks. They'd only gone out alone five times or so to drink tea, but they were already pretty much a couple.

"So, he works at an advertising company?"

Naoko couldn't back down once she saw the surprise in Kazami's eyes. Her father was indeed employed at an advertising company. During an idle period when he had no job, a friend from his night school had helped him out and given him some subcontracted work for a small printer in town. He would draft and lay out leaflet advertisements for supermarkets and similar businesses that were inserted in newspapers.

"Our prices are too low, you won't believe you're eyes!" Naoko had glared sidelong at this leaflet, grammatical errors and all, on her way to work this morning.

Naoko and Kazami were reflected in the mirrored walls. Kazami was twenty-six. During the morning rush hour he would be spit out above ground near the Ōtemachi subway station, a typical young salaryman who carried with him envelopes bearing his company's name. He wasn't exceptionally attractive, nor did he seem to have a particularly sharp mind. But he was raised with good manners, and next to Naoko that made him seem like her little brother.

Despite all her pretensions, Naoko's appearance was drab. She was ordinary-looking, and her type wasn't helped by nice makeup or nice clothes. Even when she made herself up and went to a wedding ceremony, people would often ask her afterwards, "Oh, were you there too?" Her boss had told her once when they met outside that she had the mien of a girl wearing some mundane navy blue jacket. Hers was an existence with a faint shadow and no sparkle. At twenty-seven, she had experienced nothing more than two or three bouts of unrequited love. Once she had given up hope, she began to chat a little with Kazami, who worked for a client.

Embellishing her circumstances would present large problems for Naoko down the road. She knew that if they got married, the inconsistencies would surface. But even that was all right. This very moment, right now, was precious.

One of Naoko's father's hobbies was Noh chanting, and he had made her practice it as a child. She would laugh when she practiced, so in the end he gave up and let her stop. But she told Kazami that even now she could sing a little.

She sang a bit of "Hashi Benkei" for him: "*This is Musashibō Benkei, who lives near Saitō.*"

Once she had gotten going, there was no stopping her: Naoko's mother and father were both fifty-three, and her mother had experience with both tea ceremony and flower arrangement. Perhaps because of that, her mother was strict about etiquette even now. She disdained barley tea and would say, "If you're going to drink that, you might as well use cold water to make a cup of weak green tea." Naoko showed Kazami her mother's grimace.

"Wow, that's really something." Kazami's sighs were getting louder and louder.

Naoko said that her little sister, who was almost eighteen, loved to write poems and had received a fifty-thousand-yen prize for a submission to a small magazine that won first place.

"Do you live in a condo?"

When Naoko said they lived in a house with a garden, Kazami's sigh had an extra measure of sincerity.

"And you have tatami mat rooms too?"

"Yeah."

"That's the greatest luxury these days, isn't it?"

Kazami lived in a men's dormitory. Just hearing about tatami mats and a veranda was enough to send him into a trance, he said.

"When I was a kid, I used to go to the countryside for summer vacation. I would eat watermelon sitting on the veranda, dangling my legs off the edge. I would compete with my older cousins to see who could spit the seeds the farthest."

He told Naoko that it felt good to put his feet up against the wall when he napped on the tatami mats, so he did that often. And afterward he would be scolded for the dirty, blackened spots he left on the wall in the shape of his small feet.

"Are there trees in your garden?"

"Are there any gardens without trees?"

Pine, maple, Japanese aralia. Naoko went so far as to tell him that there was even a *nanten*, a sacred bamboo plant, near the washbasin.

"A *nanten*!" Kazami closed his eyes. "It's been years since I've seen a *nanten*!"

Kazami's speech was becoming more casual and comfortable. Delighted, Naoko could feel a heat in her earlobes.

"Naoko, you live in incredible luxury." And then: "Do you own the house?"

As if it were just a matter of course, Naoko gave a small nod.

"But it's not much property."

Of course she didn't say that they were on less than eleven hundred square feet of leased land, or that they were involved in a dispute with their landlord over whether they would vacate the property. A small thorn pierced Naoko's breast, but her intoxication won out.

THERE WERE A NUMBER of other couples besides Naoko and Kazami reflected in the mirrors. How many people in that café were being truthful with each other? For a moment, Naoko had a vision of all the couples embellishing their own circumstances as they talked in that barren, shimmering white café.

"How do you feel about French tonight?"

It might have been Naoko's imagination, but she felt that Kazami's tone was more polite. Kazami was thinking of her as the daughter of an advertising executive and a woman versed in tea ceremony and flower arrangement, a young woman who lived in a wonderful house with a garden.

Naoko gave a relaxed nod. Indulging herself in the intoxication was the only way to forget her guilt. When they left the café, she linked arms with Kazami in a natural gesture. Her spine nearly dissolved in that heavy sweetness. It was the first time in Naoko's life she had experienced this feeling.

Kazami hailed a taxi.

He could invite me to a place very different from a French bistro and in my current state I'd probably go with him, thought Naoko.

Kazami politely urged her to get into the taxi before him.

"This is a tight skirt, so why don't you go in first, Honey," Naoko responded. As soon as she said it, she realized that she had called him "Honey." This time, it was the nape of her neck that immediately flushed with heat.

Somewhat affectedly, Naoko put her rear on the

seat and then began to swivel her feet and high heels into the car. Perhaps the driver was impatient—the driver-operated automatic door closed just a hair ahead of her. She exclaimed "Oh!" as pain shot through her left ankle.

KAZAMI INSISTED ON TAKING her back to her house and wouldn't take no for an answer. In comparison, the pain and swelling in Naoko's left ankle was nothing. After a quick examination at a nearby medical clinic she had been told that there was no damage to her bones and that the swelling should subside in two or three days.

She protested that she could make it home by herself, but Kazami said he was partially responsible and forced himself into the taxi with her. The scenery of the streets around them, neon lights now beginning to twinkle, rushed past the car windows like a deck of cards being shuffled. It wasn't just the French food that had drifted away. The first love Naoko had ever tasted would last only a month. She leaned on the seat in total exhaustion and stared vacantly out the window.

Once, when Naoko had just entered elementary school, she had seen a bellflower bud open with a faint popping sound. She remembered thinking then that there really must be gods in this world. Tonight, those gods were heartless. They refused to indulge her vanity and had retaliated immediately.

All she could do now was prevent the taxi from stopping in front of her house. She made up an excuse, asking the driver to stop at the lot's entrance gate. If she could keep Kazami from seeing her house she could prolong the dream just a little.

But Naoko's hopes were in vain. Kazami said that

if she walked the remaining distance she might hurt her foot.

"It's all right, we can go right in," said the driver.

The car pulled up in front of the house. Naoko felt like she was seeing her own home for the first time. The shabby, untrimmed hedges under the dim streetlamps grew entirely unchecked. Just inside the "gate"—which could barely be called that—sat a small, decaying two-story house. On the roof of the foyer were some yellowish-brown articles hanging down like seaweed. They were probably her father's undershirts, which must have fallen down from the clothesline on the second floor and been left outside in that state to weather the elements.

Just as Naoko was saying, "This is close enough," the door of the foyer opened and her mother, Sue, came out holding some bath implements. She looked at Naoko's bandaged ankle as Naoko leaned on Kazami's shoulder for support. "What happened to you?"

The chemise peeked out from under the hem of her mother's dress, a plain one-piece made of yukata cotton. She was wearing her husband's socks under slip-on sandals.

It was all over for Naoko.

At this point, going by half-measures would be worse than just taking it all the way. With a sensation that she was beating herself senseless, Naoko decided she would show Kazami the entire house and then forget about the whole thing completely.

"Won't you come in for a moment?" She intended to say it with complete cheerfulness, but at the end of the question her voice wavered a little.

KAZAMI LOOKED VERY SURPRISED, though he didn't say anything about it.

On the first floor there were a six-tatami-mat room, a four-and-a-half-mat room, and a three-mat room. On the second floor were a four-and-a-half-mat and a three-mat room. The rooms were indeed all tatami rooms, but the floor joists were deformed and since the tatami mats hadn't been changed in a number of years, they were warped and sagging, and made creaking noises when stepped on. Also, the last sliding storm door wouldn't come out of the shutter box no matter how hard she pulled.

In the mere token of a garden there were indeed pines, maples, and aralias, but they were pitiful things barely taller than a person. Kazami probably realized as much since he was standing by the washbasin, but the *nanten* was actually in the garden next door.

"We do actually have a bath, but the tiles are broken, and nowadays we always use the public bathhouse." Putting the bath implements on top of the shoe rack, Sue offered that as an excuse, but it was already futile.

Looking at her family together under the dim lights, Naoko knew that most men would take a dislike to them.

"Thank you for always looking after Naoko," said Shūji, her father. He bowed, the top of his head bald as a peeled potato, and greeted Kazami wearing a stretched-out undershirt that was barely a step up from the ones caught on the roof of the foyer. He apparently hadn't thought to throw on a shirt even though his daughter had brought home a male friend. He was a good-natured person but a poor talker, so once he was done with the greeting there was a melancholy silence.

The tea that Naoko's mother poured for them was some cheap stuff with a brown color, even less appealing than the tea they drank at work. The teacup was an indelicate thing. When her father had enjoyed a better station in life, her mother had in fact done tea ceremony and flower arrangement, but now there were tea chests piled up in the ceremonial alcove and not a single flower around. If Naoko were accused of exaggerating, she would be totally defenseless.

What brought Naoko the most embarrassment was her little sister Junko. She was a high school senior. Perhaps trying to be courteous, Kazami had chosen to talk about her winning poem.

"How did you spend the fifty-thousand-yen prize?"

Junko's face was grayish and mousy. She gave Kazami a quick upward glance.

"It wasn't fifty thousand yen." Her voice was hard and completely lacking in sweetness.

"The prize was ten thousand yen. How embarrassing—I guess I must have misled you," said Naoko.

The sushi delivery arrived.

It was a plain order, the simplest combination meal from Matsu Sushi, which was the cheapest sushi place in their modest neighborhood. Apparently the tuna hadn't fully thawed. It smelled fishy and had sherbet-like grittiness when they tasted it. That was the absolute end.

Naoko called out "Goodbye!" in a loud voice at Kazami's back as he left to go home.

Kazami bowed silently and attempted to close the sliding door to the foyer. The door didn't open and shut smoothly, and he couldn't close it on the first try. Sue stepped down onto the ground and finally managed to close it with a loud rattle.

A WEEK PASSED WITHOUT word from Kazami. Naoko had resigned herself to her fate. Of course Kazami wouldn't contact her. And yet she sensed that part of her was waiting for him. On Friday night she made overtime work for herself. It was customary for her to go out with Kazami Friday evenings.

She waited until eight o'clock, but the phone didn't ring. She could climb stairs with no problem now, but the descent was still a little painful, so Naoko returned home favoring her left leg. When she opened the gate and looked up, Naoko saw that her father's seaweed undershirts were still there. Suddenly she was furious.

"There has to be some limit to your messiness. You're so embarrassing!"

"If you're going to be bringing people here, you should say something first. Do you think I'm just playing around all day?" Naoko's mother gave as good as she got.

Sue worked a part-time job delivering yogurt drinks, so she went out on a bicycle in the morning. Working outside, her hair had become dry and frizzy, and her skin was sunburned and coarse.

"When it's this bad, it's like rubbing lotion into a tree trunk," she would sometimes say.

Sue had no beauty regimen, so if one judged only by the nape of her neck and her palms, she looked manlier than her husband when the two of them sat together. As before, she was wearing a pair of Shūji's old socks today. This time her socks had horizontal stripes.

"Would it kill you to take those off when guests come over?"

"My feet would be *brr-brr*." As she approached menopause, Sue had been saying that her feet got cold.

"What language is '*brr-brr*'?"

"What language do you think I'm speaking?"

"Seems to me like this is all on purpose," said Naoko. At this point any pretense was fine. She needed an outlet for her frustration, which had reached intolerable levels.

"Are you talking about me?"

"You'd be in trouble if I got married." Naoko was referring to her custom of contributing half of her paycheck to the family finances every month.

"We don't mind at all. Don't hold back—hurry up and find someone." Sue cut first. She was Naoko's own mother, but she stabbed deeply where her daughter didn't want anybody to go. Sue's skin wasn't the only part of her that had become coarse.

"No man will have me. As soon as he meets my parents he'll jump ship for sure."

"We're not going to be alive forever. The problem here is with your ability to attract men."

Naoko reached out toward the teacup on the low dining table. If she smashed the cup it might relieve her tension a little, but just then her father let out a dry cough as if to divert her attention.

"Your mother isn't doing this for the fun of it."

Naoko already knew what her mother would say next, if given the chance: If Shūji straightened himself out and just brought home a paycheck each month, their household and Naoko's mother herself would be fine.

Whenever the conversation reached that point,

Shūji would always take out his *go* board and start placing the stones on it. He had no luck with work. Both the economic boom of the mid-nineteen fifties and the succeeding period of rapid growth had slipped past him. There was a time when he had been able to let Sue pursue her lessons and he himself had enjoyed the freedom to learn Noh chanting, but like a rolling stone he had tumbled down and now Sue's part-time job brought in more money. And Sue's mannerisms had become as coarse as Shūji's were timid. The atmosphere in the house had become visibly rough as well.

Shūji placed the *go* stones on the board softly.

"Dad!" This time Naoko attacked her father. "Put those stones on the board with some energy!"

Just as Naoko started to say, "I hate the way you're putting them on the board," there was a voice in the foyer.

"Is anybody home?" It was Kazami.

"I had to leave for a business trip to Hokkaido right after we saw each other last time. . . ." After asking about her twisted ankle, he thrust out a big square box. "You might not like potatoes, but I brought you these."

Naoko tried to say, "I love them!" but she choked up and couldn't speak properly. She noticed that Sue, who had briefly stepped into the foyer, was now taking off her striped socks in front of the hand-washing basin.

After Kazami had gone home, Naoko pulled the seaweed-colored undershirts down from the roof of the foyer using the tip of the hose from the vacuum cleaner.

"You don't have to do that now. Can't it wait until morning?" said Sue. But Naoko couldn't wait until morning. Her little sister Junko gave her a look of contempt, but Naoko hardly even noticed.

KAZAMI BEGAN TO VISIT their house on the weekends to unwind. Naoko wanted to meet him alone, outside, but for some reason he preferred to come to the house. After they drained their mugs of beer at a beer hall, Kazami would take her home and come in with her. When Naoko offered him leftover *ochazuke* rice soup or curry rice, he ate plenty and had seconds.

"Young people nowadays have their heads screwed on right, don't they? When he eats here it doesn't cost him anything," said Sue. "What do you think his intentions are?"

Sue talked nastily behind his back, but there was proof that she wasn't as angry as she sounded: she had developed a habit on the weekends of preparing boiled root vegetables and *oden* stew fit to please any bachelor. Until Kazami started visiting she had been absorbed in her work and made do with pre-made dishes, but now the scents of food boiling in soup stock often wafted from the kitchen.

"I THOUGHT YOU WEREN'T ever going to visit me again." When she was alone with Kazami, Naoko had gone ahead and said it.

"Why?"

"Because . . . of my exaggerations."

"Any woman who isn't a bit vain isn't a woman at all."

He isn't shocked. He thinks it was cute! When Naoko was happy, her chest would grow very warm, as if she had swallowed hot water.

The summer ended, and the insects started to

make their noises in the garden and under the veranda. It was now customary for Kazami to come over on Friday nights to eat dinner. Before they knew it, he had a designated seat at the table. The seat had been Shūji's up until then. Shūji would move to an adjacent seat and offer the unopened evening paper to Kazami before reading it himself.

Kazami would sit in a comfortable cross-legged position, eat edamame and boiled taro potato skins, and drink beer at his leisure. Initially only Naoko and Sue kept him company. But the grumpy Junko, who at first would climb up to the second floor and stay there, was apparently enticed by the sounds of their conversation. Gradually, she started to come downstairs and sip a half-cup of beer. Shūji, who couldn't drink liquor, would sit in front of his token cup and raptly watch comedy programs on TV with the volume mostly muted.

Even though they were Kazami's conversation partners, neither Naoko nor Sue was particularly cheerful, nor were they skilled hosts, so the conversation wasn't very animated. And, Kazami himself being a man of few words, there were breaks in the dialogue. Naoko worried about it at first, but soon she realized she was being overanxious.

"When I come here I can really relax. When you're listening to the sounds of computers all day, some time to just zone out is a real treat. That, and the smell here is great. Just like a house in the country, the smell of dried bonito."

"Isn't that just the smell of an old house?" asked Sue.

"Nowadays that's precious. Wherever you go now there's always that ammonia smell from synthetic building material that stings your eyes."

When Kazami finished eating, he would say, "Excuse me," and with that he would push himself back from the table, sprawl on the tatami mats, and breathe deeply. The floorboards were as loose as they'd always been, but underneath Kazami's body, on top of the old, yellowish-brown tatami mats, there was a patterned rush mat. The tea chests were gone from the ceremonial alcove, and there was a flower in a cheap bud vase. The lightbulb in the living room was brighter now.

"Kazami, Naoko says you're an only child."

WHILE SUE TALKED WITH him, Naoko noticed that her mother's face was reflected in the base of the black tea caddy. Naoko realized that Sue was gently pressing the pads of her fingers around her oily nostrils. It was the first time Naoko had ever seen her mother do that. Sue's simple one-piece dress hadn't changed, but her hair was tied up neatly and she had given up the men's socks in favor of bare feet.

When Naoko asked, "Mom, aren't your feet going *brr-brr*?" her mother responded, "Maybe I feel better because I've had a little beer. It seems like my circulation has improved."

It had been countless years since Naoko had heard her speak like that. Among the circle of women working part-time jobs, Sue said, any woman who spoke in a refined manner would seem like she was putting on airs and be ostracized. So Sue had adopted a rough diction.

Perhaps because of her job delivering small packages of yogurt drinks, the way Sue placed small dishes on the table also used to be rough. But nowadays, she would put them down noiselessly.

When everything's said and done, she is my mother

after all, thought Naoko. *She's doing everything she can to avoid causing her daughter any more embarrassment.*

JUNKO STOOD UP ABRUPTLY and left.

If she's going upstairs to study, she should say a word to Kazami, thought Naoko. But Junko came right back. She had gone into the adjacent room to get a cushion. With an angry expression, she placed the cushion, folded in half, near Kazami's head and shot out of the room again. For Junko, this kind of behavior was as much as anyone could hope for.

When Kazami came over, the house became visibly brighter. Only Shūji was left out.

THE WALL CLOCK IN the living room struck eight.

"He's late, isn't he?" Sue looked up at the clock.

Naoko and Junko, following their mother's lead, looked up at it too.

"Naoko, did you and Kazami get into a fight?"

"Why would I do that?" Naoko was never left alone with him, so how could they possibly fight?

Kazami always came on Friday between six-thirty and seven, but today he hadn't shown up or contacted them at all. Sitting in front of the fully prepared dinner table, the three women looked up at the clock and worried.

"I hope he wasn't in some kind of car accident."

"Stop it, Mom. You shouldn't say things like that."

After all their worrying about Kazami, they suddenly realized that Shūji was missing too.

A little before six, Shūji had said, "I'm going out to get some cigarettes," and then left the house.

Kazami was coming over, so Shūji must have been going out to buy a pack of Cabin cigarettes.

Kazami had run out of cigarettes once and Shūji had given Kazami one of his Seven Stars. Sue said to him later, "You don't have to worry about anything else, so would you please just take care of Kazami's cigarettes?" And ever since he had fulfilled the duty faithfully.

"He might have stopped to play pachinko somewhere along the way."

"But for two hours?"

Junko interrupted them: "I wonder if he's run away?"

"Run away?"

Junko pulled off the cloth that was covering the food on the dinner table, and while she was sampling a side dish with her fingers, she said, "We're always talking about Kazami this and Kazami that. That can't be much fun for Dad."

It was true. If they got the first matsutake mushrooms of the season, they would wait to eat them until Kazami came over. And to make matters worse, these days they treated the subdued Shūji like he was a freeloader in the house.

"If Dad were the kind of person who had enough guts to run away, then Mom wouldn't be having such a hard time," said Naoko.

Sue looked up at the wall clock again. She stood up and moved toward the kitchen. "Wow, he's really late."

Junko also stood up and went over to the foyer, apparently to have a look outside. Naoko was left in the living room alone.

Mom and Junko are more worried about him than I am, she thought. It didn't exactly disturb her, but she felt a little strange, as if what was rightfully hers had been snatched away.

After all that horrible worrying, the two men came to the house together a little after ten o'clock.

"We're here!"

At Kazami's shout and the knocking on the glass door to the foyer, the three women flew over to him. Kazami was carrying Shūji on his back, swaying as he stood. Shūji was dead drunk.

"We ran into each other in front of the train station. It was a total coincidence so he suggested we go for a quick drink."

While Kazami explained that they had gone to a *yakitori* restaurant and gotten carried away in their drinking, he helped Sue carry Shūji—limp like a broken marionette—into bed.

"A coincidence? Yeah right. I bet Shūji ambushed him, thinking he could have Kazami all to himself. . . ." As she was complaining, the observant Sue noticed some filth on Kazami's trousers. "What happened to your pants?"

There was some dried vomit around the crotch of Kazami's pants. It had caught Naoko's eye immediately, but she had failed to mention it for some reason.

"Shūji got sick on our way back."

"Oh, I'm so sorry. Please, put on a yukata. I'll clean these up right now. Naoko, get a yukata for Kazami!" Sue was in command.

Kazami went out onto the veranda, put on the yukata, and took off his pants. The intoxication seemed to hit him all at once. He leaned against the wall and began to nod off.

Kazami wound up spending the night. They laid out Sue's bedding next to Shūji and let Kazami sleep there. It was the six-mat room next to the living room, and they could still hear the two men snoring even after they shut the thick sliding doors tight.

Naoko and Junko began a late dinner, eating the food Sue had prepared. Next to them, Sue cleaned Kazami's pants.

Naoko complained in a quiet voice, "You shouldn't do that right next to people having a meal."

What she really wanted to say was, "Shouldn't I be the one taking care of Kazami's needs?" but it was difficult for her to put it directly.

"Say what you will, but if I don't do this quickly it'll seep into the fabric and then it won't ever come out." Sue diligently smacked the grimy area using a cloth she had moistened with warm water, and then she put an iron to it. There was a sizzle when she laid the hot iron on the wet spots, and a sour, oily smell rose up. It was the smell of a young man, a smell absent from this house. Junko was eating casually with her chopsticks, but Naoko immediately saw that her sister was also conscious of the smell. Every time Sue changed the position of the iron, there was the smell. With a serious expression, Sue licked her index finger and put it to the iron to test the temperature.

Naoko had thought that the thick downy hair that grew on her mother's upper lip had simply turned white, but when she looked closer she realized that it was now gone. Her mother's formerly connected eyebrows were now nicely shaped. Apparently Sue had taken a razor to her facial hair.

"Hey, Kazami! Hey, Kazami!" Shūji was talking in his sleep. His tone was familiar and supplicating. Up until then he hadn't participated in their conversations and simply had watched TV alone, so what did he and Kazami have to talk about all night long? Once again, Naoko had a sense that her proper share of something had been taken from her.

After she finished with the iron, Sue started to get up, saying, "Oh, that's right—I'd better put some water by their bedsides. Those poor guys."

"I'll do it." Naoko stood up a moment before her mother and poured some water from the kitchen into a teakettle. She put two cups on a tray with the kettle and brought them back to the table.

"Yes, thank you."

Sue took the tray nonchalantly and went into the neighboring room. Junko, chewing silently on a pickled radish, looked up at her sister's face. Naoko didn't show it, but once again she felt like what was rightly hers had been usurped.

They didn't have an extra bed, so that night Sue and Naoko shared a futon. They lay next to each other, back to back, but after Sue closed her eyes she rolled over.

Naoko was surprised. "Mom," she said in a low voice. "Mom, are you using my makeup?" Recently Naoko's makeup had been depleting very quickly. She'd suspected Junko, but it seemed like Sue was the culprit.

Instead of answering, Sue gave a single yawn and her breath soon took on the rhythm of sleep.

IT WAS EITHER TUESDAY or Wednesday evening when Naoko dropped by Kazami's office. She didn't have any particular business with him. In another two or three days it would be Friday and Kazami would come over to her house for dinner, but she wanted the two of them to be alone occasionally. She was also feeling a little lonely because she never heard a word from him except on Fridays.

When Naoko went to the reception desk and asked for Kazami five minutes before the end of the workday, the receptionist said he was already downstairs in a coffee shop with a visitor.

"Is it a client from work?"

"No, it's a young woman."

It was like being lashed with a whip. Was this why Kazami wouldn't meet with her except on Fridays?

Naoko started to head home then, but after thinking it over, she decided that her habit of reacting this way was why things never worked out for her. She might as well see the woman's face before heading back. She peeked into the café in the basement of the building and was shocked by what she saw.

In front of Kazami sat Junko. There were two classmates from her literature club with her, one of them a boy. On the table was the newest issue of one of the specialized magazines that was popular with the young people.

"They took another one of my poems. But I was just a runner-up this time, so I only got a thousand yen." Junko said that she had come to see a movie in the neighborhood, so she figured she might as well drop by and show the poem to Kazami.

When Junko ate shortcake, as she was doing now, she looked like a child. But being accompanied on either side by a boy and a girl, and sitting with her legs crossed as she was, she was absolutely an adult. At home, she spoke in a soft voice, but today she was unusually cheerful. Perhaps because her cheeks were flushed, even her face—the face that Naoko thought was so very mousy—appeared womanly. Naoko hadn't realized it until now, but Junko's chest and hips had filled out as well.

"When I came down I thought that it was just Jun here alone, but it's three of you. I can't charge this one to the company." Grumbling though he was,

Kazami looked like he was enjoying himself. And on top of that, at some point he had started calling her "Jun."

He opened the magazine and looked for Junko's poem. It had themes of love and sex, a terribly abstract piece.

Junko's brought her classmates along with her because she's proud of her sister's boyfriend, thought Naoko. And yet she once again experienced a strange feeling, like a portion of her stockholdings had been transferred to someone else's name.

RECORDED FESTIVAL MUSIC HAD been playing in the neighborhood since the morning.

Up until then Naoko's family hadn't paid any mind to festivals. They hadn't donated anything, nor would they hang the sacred lanterns or partake in the sacred sake, but this year they changed their tune. There were now lanterns swaying by the gate and near the newly trimmed hedges, though the trimming was obviously amateur work.

It wasn't a Friday but it was a special occasion, so they had invited Kazami over. He came over in the evening and was surprised to see a new festival yukata laid out for him. But Naoko was even more surprised than Kazami. This was the first time Sue had done anything like this. She always refused to do anything that required money or time, as Naoko knew from years of living with her in the same house.

But there wasn't a new yukata for everybody in the family.

"Shūji doesn't like festivals." Shūji was the only one left out.

"It's more relaxing to stay home and watch the

house anyway," said Shūji, as if it were only natural. "Go and take your time," he said as he took out his *go* board and began to place the stones on it.

The three women, having changed into their yukata, encircled Kazami as they all walked through the jostling festival crowd. Both Sue and Junko laughed plenty. A goldfish-catching game that Naoko didn't think was very interesting became something more when Kazami joined in.

Junko bought some grilled squid, and Kazami bought an *oden* dish, miso spread onto skewered triangular cuts of devil's tongue. He seemed to be nostalgic for the food, and they walked while they ate. Taking advantage of the crowd, Naoko put her arm through Kazami's and stuck by his side. In part, she wanted her mother and sister to see it.

Kazami had been jostled by the crowd and also wasn't used to wearing traditional clothes. As a result, his yukata had come open at the hem, giving him a sloppy appearance.

"What's going on with your yukata? You look like a little kid."

Laughing, Sue pulled Kazami into a dark spot behind a row of vegetable stands. She untied and unwound his belt and then nimbly retied it.

"There. Now stand up straight. All right, let's go!"

As if he were a child, Sue smacked Kazami—who was a head taller than she was—on the butt. Soon after that was when the incident occurred.

At one point while the four of them were walking bunched together, being pushed by the waves of people, Sue suddenly let out a shriek. It sounded like the bright voice of a younger woman.

"How old does he think I am? I'm fifty-three! Fifty-three!"

Some man in the crowd had fondled Sue.

"He has some nerve, touching me like that, but he must be new at this! It's not like I was walking down a street alone at night. There are these two young women with me, so why would he choose my fifty-three-year-old butt over theirs?"

Laughing like a cooing pigeon, she repeated, "That guy just doesn't have an eye for women."

Kazami, Naoko, and Junko all laughed a little for her benefit.

There were traces of makeup on Sue's flushed cheeks. Her perfume, its scent noticeable in the heat, wasn't something she had taken from Naoko's dresser. Sue was buying beauty products herself, something she hadn't done for years and years.

BACK AT HOME, SUE was wearing her matching, tie-dyed yukata loosely to show as much skin as possible. She poured beer for Kazami, and for Naoko and Junko too. Again, she let out a cooing laugh.

"Sure it was a festival, but with my daughters right there—it's embarrassing. How old did he think I was? I'm fifty-three. Fifty-three!"

"Stop saying that over and over!" yelled Shūji. He had been lining his *go* stones up out on the veranda when he suddenly chastised Sue in a startlingly loud voice.

"Give it a rest." The veins near his temples were bulging. His hand—the one holding the *go* pieces—was shaking.

"Stop it. He's just jealous." Perhaps in an attempt to save the soured atmosphere, Sue jocularly tried to smooth things over and poured another round of beer for everyone. "Who's behaving childishly now?" she said.

When Sue called him jealous, Naoko noticed that despite Shūji's potato-shaped head, his expression was indeed a masculine one. This wasn't the usual timid Shūji who humored Sue and was solicitous of Kazami. Naoko felt a new awareness that her parents really were a married couple.

Naoko also realized something else. The interior of their house seemed bright and lively as festival music drifted in on the night wind. Their slovenly home was now all neatened up. There was a chrysanthemum in the ceremonial alcove, and the beer glasses weren't complimentary gifts from the liquor store but rather cut glass, fit for guests. The pine, maple, and aralia in the garden seemed healthier, maybe because the lighting in the tatami rooms was brighter. Of course there was no *nanten* by the washbasin, but the hand towel fluttering in the wind over there was brand new.

Outside was an autumn festival and cool air too chilly for yukata, but inside the house spring had finally arrived.

Spring has come. Spring has come.

Where has it come?

To the mountains, to the villages, to the fields.

Naoko thought of the popular children's song.

Spring had come, not just for Sue, but for Shūji, and for Junko too, gloomy as she used to be. For everyone. Perhaps feeling that his shouting had been childish, Shūji put down his *go* stones, came over and poured beer for Kazami.

"Dad, looks like you want to join us." Kazami then poured for Shūji while Shūji held the glass.

Sue looked at Kazami and said softly, "When we're all together like this, we really are a family, aren't we?" Then her tone became a little more formal. "Kazami, maybe I went too far there?"

Naoko nearly choked. She didn't think Sue would bring it up this way, not at a time like this. Kazami squinted a little, and after looking at the three women, he nodded his head briskly. Sue and Junko, and then Naoko, released their stifled breath audibly.

"Well, how about next spring?"

The froth from the beer that Sue poured into Kazami's glass was all but overflowing.

Shūji looked at the three women one by one, then said in a low voice, "You've really got your work cut out for you."

THE EVENING OF THE following Thursday, Naoko was waiting for Kazami in the café. Her expectant face was reflected in the mirrors. It was the same café where she had carelessly exaggerated, saying that her father was an executive at an advertising company and that her mother was versed in tea ceremony and flower arrangement.

Even putting her vanity aside, Naoko felt that she really had become a bit more womanly and lively than before. Her clothes, too, were no longer the mousy brown things she had worn then. More than anything, the composure that came from knowing she had a partner appeared to add a gloss to her hair and skin from within.

Kazami came in. Naoko waited for him to light his cigarette and then she started to speak.

"I'd like you to come over for dinner every other week instead of every week like you've been doing."

Kazami started to say something, but Naoko ignored him and continued. She knew she was a poor talker, but she just had to get this out.

"When you come over, we always do everything as a family. But we can wait until after the marriage to do the family stuff. Come to think of it, we've never really eaten and talked as a couple."

Kazami was silent for a short while. The two of them, sitting face to face, were reflected in the mirrors.

"There's something I really should have told you before." Kazami exhaled cigarette smoke. "I don't know if it's because my blood type is AB, but I'm a really indecisive person." He avoided Naoko's eyes and looked at the mirrors.

"Our engagement . . ." Then Kazami bowed his head briefly. "I've lost my self-confidence. It's too much for me to take on."

Those were the two reasons.

Naoko stared dumbly at the mirrors. Somehow, she had sensed this was coming ever since that day when she had put on airs and embellished her circumstances. When Shūji had looked at the women one by one and said, "You've really got your work cut out for you," had he meant that Kazami would be taking on three brides at once?

There were a number of couples reflected in the mirrors. As if she were an unrelated observer, Naoko thought, *Now there's a couple that's being honest about their true feelings.*

SHE WALKED SLOWLY FROM the train station back to her house. Why had Kazami come over every week even though he didn't have any intention of getting married? Did he feel pity for Naoko and her pretensions?

Bulging, brown tatami mats over loose floorboards. He had said it smelled like bonito flakes.

Did he find the age and grime relaxing? Was this gloomy and ineloquent household more comfortable for him than an elite family? He had said he was an only child, so maybe he was happy to have a mother and sister around.

When Naoko opened the door to the foyer in a daze, Junko rushed over to her.

"Mom's acting weird," she said with a tense expression.

Sue was crouching in front of the dresser in the living room. On top of her usual Western-style clothes she was wearing a new formal black kimono and squeezing her head.

"It feels like my head's going to split in half," she said and then crumpled forward, collapsing. She lost consciousness immediately. It was a subarachnoid hemorrhage. After three days of unconsciousness, it was over.

The kimono was a cheap thing that Sue had just picked out at a department store before her collapse. This formal kimono, which she had bought with her pin money all too soon, became Sue's shroud when they put her in her coffin.

AFTER THE MEMORIAL SERVICE, Naoko bumped into Kazami in front of Ōtemachi Station.

"Oh." Kazami raised his hand awkwardly. "Is everyone doing well?"

Naoko started to say, "In fact, my mom—" but then she shut her mouth. It was thanks to this man that spring had come to her house, even if it had been brief. For a while people had been saying to her, "Naoko, what have you been doing lately? You really look great these days." Even Junko, an obstinate bud, had blossomed. Her cowardly father had become manly, and her mother had become womanly.

Naoko was surprised when she opened her mother's dresser to put on Sue's funeral makeup. There was new lipstick and face powder inside. In her formal kimono and with her makeup applied heavily, Sue was beautiful, as if she were just leaving for her daughter's wedding.

"We're doing well. We're all doing well." Naoko wanted her mother to live a little longer within Kazami.

"Oh yeah? I hope your mom hasn't had to deal with any more molesters."

"The festival's over now, so I think she'll be fine."

"I guess so."

Kazami laughed, and Naoko laughed a little too.

"Goodbye!" Naoko's voice was so loud it surprised even her.

Contributors

the author

Mukōda Kuniko (向田邦子; November 28, 1929–August 22, 1981) was born in Tokyo, Japan. After graduating Jissen Women's Educational Institute, she began work at film publicity company Ondori Company in 1952. She quit in 1960 to write for the screen and radio, winning the 1980 Naoki Prize for her short stories "Hanano Namae," "Kawauso," and "Inugoya." Those stories and ten others were published in English translation in *The Name of the Flower* (ISBN 978-1880656-09-9) by Stone Bridge Press, in 1994.

Mukōda died unexpectedly in an aircraft disaster in Taiwan.

the translator

A. Reid Monroe-Sheridan is a corporate lawyer and Associate Professor at Keio University Law School in Tokyo. He has previously taught courses at the University of Tokyo Graduate Schools for Law and Politics and Hitotsubashi University Graduate School of International Corporate Strategy. He holds a B.A. in Japanese literature from Carleton College and a J.D. from Harvard Law School and is a graduate of the Inter-University Center for Japanese Language Studies based in Yokohama.

the artist

Ramona Russu is Romanian artist based in the South of France. Since the beginnings of her artistic career, Ramona developed a very personal style which combines her admiration for the female silhouette with her passion for a graphic and monochrome aesthetic.

With her subtle, sensitive yet strong female portraits, Ramona Russu manages to captivate the viewer by telling a visual story about 'The girl with black hair' in a surreal, graphic and poetic style.

Ramona's pieces are a perfect balance between pure decoration and genuine emotion. Listed in various private collections across Europe, America and Asia, her works have been exhibited in many solo and group exhibitions and international art fairs.

Her art has also been featured in magazines like Forbes, Art & Décoration, Harper's Bazaar and Saatchi Fall Catalog. In 2019 Ramona's works have been selected to represent The Annual Fall Gallery Walk in Chicago on FOX News.

Her works may be viewed at ramonarussu.com and on Instagram @ramona_russu